PA

Paul Tippet

OLD
MRS. LONELY
KNOWS

outskirts
press

Outskirts Press, Inc.
http://www.outskirtspress.com

ISBN: 978-1-9772-3253-3

Outskirts Press and the "OP" logo are trademarks belonging to Outskirts Press, Inc.

PRINTED IN THE UNITED STATES OF AMERICA

Dedication

For Kathleen Kaminski, Dear Friend and Mentor

CHAPTER 1

She awoke in the dark, her mind totally blank as to her identity, her location and what bed she found herself in. For she was in a bed, there was something quite soft beneath her and there was a distinct feeling that she could easily begin to fall, to spiral downward into a dark hole from which there was never a coming back. Her head seemed to be spinning and her stomach felt as though it were about to let go of whatever food or drink it held. And it was cold, so cold that her shaking hand seemed to be searching for something to pull around her for warmth.

And then suddenly she became aware of a roaring sound, one that seemed to rise to a crescendo and then fall and rise again. It became suddenly quite loud, the very air around her seemed to vibrate with sound and from somewhere there was a rattling of a wall or a window and then a kind of crash as though something had fallen against whatever building she was in. A sense of sudden fear and dread washed over her then and her heart began to beat erratically, as though it was about to escape from her chest. She knew at once that she was having a dreaded anxiety attack, and with the onslaught of the attack her identity returned to her in a rush, along with the feeling that she was dying and was about to take her last breath.

That sense of the mind coming alive again suddenly after sleep was always bad enough on its own, but doubled with the shock of anxiety, Kathleen Longley, felt as though she were about to go mad. She instinctively reached out for the bedside lamp, fumbling for it with a shaking hand in the dark. She found the switch but when she managed to turn it nothing happened. The pitch blackness seemed even blacker and the roaring sound that seemed to surround her became even more intense. She realized that the sound was the wind from outside. But she couldn't be sure how much of it came from the erratic beating of her own heart. The cold of the room only seemed to emphasize the physical sensations she was experiencing.

It was obvious that the electricity had gone off in the night. The whole electrical system had shut down, including the furnace. There had been warnings on the radio and television for the last couple of days of an intense winter storm that was headed toward Pennsylvania, and Bridgetown lay right in its crosshairs. But she had been nearly like a sleep walker for the past few months, and her drug of choice, alcohol, most notably wine, had for the most part kept the dreaded anxiety at bay. She had gone to bed the night before well under its influence and power, and could half remember stumbling up the stairs, humming an old love song that had haunted her all through the previous day. Now nearly sober again, sensitized to the max from the storm and the anxiety attack, trapped by the darkness, she felt completely helpless and alone. She was suddenly shaking uncontrollably and having no power to stop herself, she began to weep.

Was it possible that only the year before she had

slept through such storms, only waking occasionally when the wind rose to the highest decibels? Of course, Fred, her beloved husband had lain next to her then, warmly and comfortably in the bed they had shared for 25 years. No matter what have might happened, he was there with his steady nerves and caring heart to handle it and reassure her that all would be well. And then came the morning when she awoke to bright spring sun and birdsong, and, looking forward to breakfast and a day in the garden, was about to kiss him awake, only to find him very still and cold. He had died during the night, peacefully, without warning, at the early age of fifty-five. Kath had been fifty-four. It was as though a freight train had appeared from nowhere and sent her spinning along the tracks of her life and into an unknown country without a road sign or a map.

They had had a good life together for those years, twenty of them had been spent in Bridgetown, after they moved from New Jersey when Kath had taken a job as an English Professor at Anderson College. Fred had always been a firefighter and in Bridgetown had worked his way into a position as Fire Chief at one of the local fire stations. Their lives had been blessed, until changes had been made with Kath's job at the college. A new department head had been appointed, a Mr. Robert Sterner, a fortyish know it all who took an obviously dislike of her, out of plain meanness or jealousy, and when she could take no more of his deceit and micromanaging, had decided to take an early retirement. Fred had been totally supportive and at first the change had been an ideal one. They spent nearly a year of bliss together until Fred's sudden an unexpected death.

And now on this February night, still lost in an unknown country without him, she hoped that death would come and take her away from the horrible reality of life as she found it. She could suddenly hardly breathe and was choked by her tears and the bitter reflux from her stomach. The anxiety, at its peak, brought her hands to her throat. As she usually did at such moments, she tried to remember the instructions given by the author of a book she had read recently, one that had explained in real terms how to deal with an anxiety attack such as she was experiencing now. It explained how one's own fear kept the anxiety alive and gave subtle instructions on how to face what was happening, and how to drift past it, by facing, accepting and allowing it to pass.

She began to pray then as she sometimes did when she was in the throes of an attack as severe as the current one. She was not a religious woman and rarely attended church services. But she was deeply spiritual and believed in God. But for her God was not an angry gray-haired man standing on a mountain with a sword in his hand. To her God was love, a force and a power without form and shape. No one knew for certain the identity of God, not the pastor of the local church, not the pope or any of the highest ranked individuals in the hierarchy of the world's greatest religions. Perhaps that was only her own speculation, but somehow it had always comforted her to think that the God in her mind had a heart that was always open and ears that never failed to listen, especially at moments like this.

"Dear Father," she whispered now. "Please let me die, right this minute. I don't want to face another day or night in this awful place."

Her body was wracked with sobs once again, only these caused her entire body to shake and she grabbed unto the blankets with both hands, as though to anchor herself in the blackness.

"If I am to die, God, you will have to take a hand in the process. I am too much of a coward to do the deed myself. I've tried it before with pills and alcohol. I even took my husbands hand gun from his dresser drawer a couple of times, but my hands shook so bad I didn't even attempt to touch the trigger. So just stop my heart from this terrible beating and let me die here and now!"

She waited, lying there expectantly, but nothing happened. Her heart seemed to beat even faster and from outside the wind lashed at the house and threatened to burst her ear drums.

"If you want me to continue living," she prayed again, after lying there for several moments in her dark hole of hopelessness and panic, "then you will have to give me some sort of a sign. Take this terrible affliction of anxiety away. Give me something to live for. Give me a purpose and let me live again in peace."

After several moments of lying there amidst the roaring from outside and the roaring in her own head, the anxiety that had overcome her began to relax its grip. She sometimes thought of it as though it were a faucet turned on, and just as quickly would be turned off. Only so much water could come through at any one time. Perhaps the whole system would shut down at some point but once again she felt as though the height of the storm had been reached and a switch had been turned off.

She lay there for a time in a kind of stupor, weary and worn out, with only the deep sense of depression that usually followed the attacks lying over her like an extra heavy blanket. What in the world could she do, how could she continue to survive the severity and violence of her affliction? Her doctor had given her a prescription for an anxiety drug. She kept the bottle on her nightstand and reached for it now, fumbling in the dark. It always seemed to her that she never thought to take a pill when she was at the beginning of an attack. Only when it had reached a peak did she reach for the pills. She was able to uncap the container now, take out a pill and shove it under her tongue. The taste was awful, but the relief seemed to come quicker that way.

And it did come, slowly creeping into her legs and arms, and then up her back, a slow relaxing of her muscles. Even her hands that had been drawn into fists opened and she could move her fingers again, painfully at first, and then the pain subsided, and her hands lay flatly across her chest. Lastly, the ball of troubled thoughts that had accumulated in her head began to let go, like a bunch of rubber bands. One after another they fell away, and the ball separated and morphed into a flat rubber sheet. She lay there as the slow relaxation took over. She had no idea of how or when it happened, but she suddenly began thinking of flowers, remembering the pleasure she used to feel in Spring when she began filling the pots on the patio and the flower beds at the front and sides of the house with the geraniums and the coleus she loved, along with the impatiens, marigolds and zinnias. There were others that she cherished as well. She had once belonged to the local garden club and after she had left her career as an English professor at the local college, she had intended to continue her involvement with the club. But then her husband died, and the pots and beds remained empty, except for the weeds that had sprung up over the following summer. But now in the sudden dream like state she picked a rose from one of the bushes that lined the sides of her garage. It was a pink one, her favorite, and the scent rose to her nostrils and brought the joy of spring and the planting season to her heart and mind once again. She lifted the rose to her lips, but before it could touch it was snatched from her hand by an angry woman!

Kathleen, or Kath as she preferred to be called, recognized the woman at once. It was Geraldine Harvey, an elderly woman who lived in a small white house at the top of her street. In the dream the lady was speaking to her. She recognized the speech impediment that caused her words to come out garbled at times, their meanings often blurred. In fact, for as long as she could remember she had been referred to by Mrs. Harvey as Mrs. Lonely. And now in the dream like state she found herself in, the only words she could hear or recognize were, "You think you know everything, Mrs. Lonely!" But the tone of the words was angry, shrill, and the last thing she thought of before sinking into a drugged sleep was why in the world the old woman seemed to hate her so much.

Sometime later, a long time it seemed, she awoke to silence and a light which filled the room when she opened her eyes. The light came from the bedside lamp. The electricity had obviously come on during the early hours.

The air seemed a bit warmer around her. She felt at once the weakness that lingered from the panic of the night before, that along with the hungover feeling from all the wine she had consumed, made her want to throw up. Her mouth was so dry she could barely breath, and finally, with some effort, she was able to sit up and let her legs slide over the edge of the bed. It took a moment for her to stop the kind of spinning in her head and regain her balance, and finally while reaching out for support from the dresser and the wall and the door frame, she made her way into the adjoining bathroom. Once inside she closed the door quietly and carefully, as she might have done when her husband was still alive, so that she wouldn't awaken him. She turned on the cold-water faucet gently, plunging her shaking hand into the flow, then raising the freezing liquid to her face and eyes. Peering at herself in the mirror above the sink then, she was shocked by her appearance. She recognized the face, she had glimpsed it in the glass often enough. Once upon a time she had been calmed by the serenity that was naturally present in her. She had never been beautiful, her husband had often told her she was, but she knew he had been referring to the beauty within. She was gentle and kind, he often told her. She herself had always thought of herself as pretty. At a younger age her blond hair had billowed around a face that was nearly perfectly proportioned with a nice nose and full lips. She had never suffered from problem skin, lines or wrinkles.

The face that stared back at her now was witch like, hard and filled with terror. The skin was splotchy with spidery lines here and there. Her hair, limp and nearly all gray now, hung around her shoulders in all directions and looked as though it had never been touched by a comb. Her eyes were puffy and swollen, her lips were no longer pink. They seemed black and blue now, as though she had bitten them as she often did during her moments of extreme panic.

Shocked by her appearance, she held onto the sink while the anxiety of the night before came back to her in a rush. These days it seemed that even a thought could bring on the terror and she had no control over any of it. Her body no longer belonged to her and only wine and the dreaded medication gave her some semblance of normality. As she stumbled back into the bedroom to find her robe, she remembered there was a last bottle of wine in the refrigerator downstairs. She had brought it up from the basement the previous afternoon along with the two others she had consumed the night before. Her husband had been a connoisseur of fine wine and had luckily left many bottles of it on shelves in his personal wine cellar. Over the months since his death she had consumed quite a few bottles of his prized collection. As the anxiety attacks had increased, she had become nearly housebound. It had been months since she had taken the car out of the garage, so she hadn't been able to go to the liquor store at the other end of town to replenish her supply. She had not even gone out to buy groceries. Luckily there was a small market a couple of blocks away that was privately owned and had a delivery service. She would call the store a couple of times a week and her order would be delivered the same day. She would not even have to face the delivery man at the door. Luckily, she knew the owner of the store personally, so the billing could be done easily through her checking account or charge card. All of that was good in a way that she didn't have to go out anywhere. The thought of being caught in a checkout line at a grocery store caused her heart to pound in her chest and a dark cloud of fear to descend.

Agoraphobia was the name they gave to the affliction she suffered. Anxiety grown into a monster from which there was no escape. Even the alcohol that she had depended on for relief no longer had the same effect. She had reached a point as she had done the night before that one bottle was not enough and another one would have to be uncorked. And now on this stark morning she was already planning on a trip to the refrigerator. Before breakfast, before any food could be ingested, she needed a glass of wine to calm the inner demon.

She stumbled out of the bathroom and stood in the hallway looking down the stairs. The terror of facing the day was almost more than she could bear. Perhaps she should call 911 and just tell the ambulance driver when he came for her that he should just deliver her to the door of the nearest insane asylum, for she was certain this was where she would eventually end up. If she tried going down the stairs just now, she would lose her balance and end up a broken heap in the lower hallway. She needed the wine but the longer she stood there the more terror that rose in her. Her hands shook, and she began to sob. She suddenly thought of the pills that still sat on the nightstand and she made her way back and sat down on the edge of the bed. The cap was still off the container from the night before, but with her hands so out of control, it was still very difficult getting two of the pills into her hand and then into her mouth.

She swallowed them, half choking, and then lay back on the bed. She lay there shaking for a few moments and then as she usually did, she began to relax, slowly at first and then more quickly. She still felt ill, quite sick in the stomach, and her head throbbed. But the awful feeling of dread lifted from her, leaving her exhausted and weary but still able to breathe. She knew from experience that the pills did work eventually. But why was she so afraid of the medication? Was it a fear of becoming addicted to it? That was certainly a possibility. She had been taught since childhood, by her mother who been raised in one of the strict religious sects that were rampant in the state, that any illness should be faced with herbs and natural medicine, and faith, of course, and prayer. That was all one needed. Alcohol was never mentioned positively or negatively, since her father was prone to the bottle, and she had often found him alone somewhere drunk and passed out. Her mother knew her husband was a secret alcoholic, Kath was sure, but she lived her life around him, never acknowledging a real problem existed. But it was her own husband who taught Kath that alcohol could be used for relaxation. Properly administered it could bring relaxation and a shared joy. When mixed with food and music, wine could add to the true enjoyment of life. Perhaps that's was why when the sensitization and dreaded anxiety came upon her, she turned to the alcohol. She looked at is as a friend and a kind of confidant, a buffer for the stress that suddenly consumed her.

Now, thanks to the pills, she had come to a kind of oasis. The anxiety still lay around her waiting to strike, but it had moved back a bit, allowing some light to come into the darkness of her mind giving her some breathing room. It suddenly occurred to Kath that all was quiet around her. A strange silence had descended somehow after the fury of last night's storm. She had to make her way downstairs and see what damage had been done by the wind. She remembered the crash she had heard, but now there wasn't the slightest hint that anything was wrong outside.

Feeling more in control, though still unsteady and weak, she slid her legs off the bed and stood up slowly. She quickly glanced at the clock on the nightstand and saw that it was 730 AM. Light was coming from the two windows in the room, but it was a kind of weak winter light. There was no real sunlight as the sun itself was obviously still hidden under layers of clouds. She slowly made her way to the window that faced the back of her property and pulled the curtain aside. Outside she could see nothing but snow. Her garage and shed were covered by it, two white bulks on the winter landscape, recognizable only by the dark squares of windows. Beyond her garden the white stretched away toward the township park, nearly obscured now by snow and mist. A lingering wind still kicked up snow which blew across her field of vision, and down below, and closer to the house, a tree had fallen. It was one of the maple trees that lined Park Street that ran by the one side of her house. That was obviously the crash she had heard in the dark.

The snow and the fallen tree only helped to alarm and frighten her. She felt even more isolated and vulnerable. How was she going to deal with it all? But amazingly the power of the pill still held, keeping the anxiety at bay, she was able to get dressed in a pair of slacks and a warm sweater and slowly make her way down the stairs. She went into the living room, after switching on the light, and slowly made her way to the large picture window and with some trepidation pulled the curtains aside. Although there was still no direct sunlight coming through the darkness of the clouds, she was momentarily blinded by the brightness of the snow. When she did regain her sight, she was shocked by the view that lay before her. It had been days since she last opened the window curtains, but now her familiar world lay buried in snow. Bridge Street, that ran in front of her house, was nothing more than a white expanse. Obviously, the plows had not even come near the neighborhood and she wondered when they would be even able to come. Once again, she felt trapped and isolated and her heart began to pound. Leaning against the window seat she closed her eyes and tried breathing deeply. After a moment she felt a bit calmer and opened her eyes to the white canvas before her. This time she was able to notice details beyond the snow-covered expanse. One dark line crossed her vision. Of course, it was Anderson's Creek that ran along Bridge Street for a couple of blocks, then turned at Anderson's hill which blocked its course, dissected the town and ran south toward the river. Old man Anderson had founded the town and had built a mill nearby. Beyond the stream tall green pines rose up. Half covered by snow now she saw tufts of white begin to drop into the stream. Luckily, Anderson Creek lay deep enough in its bed that it didn't cause flooding as it passed in front of her house. Only once that she could remember did it ever rise to the street before her and cause any anxiety. The mill itself had been destroyed in a long-ago flood, but somewhere mid-century the town's name had been changed from Anderson's Mill to Bridgetown, obviously due to the twelve bridges that crossed the stream at various places as it ran through the town.

The main bridge was the huge railroad bridge that crossed the street about a block beyond her house. She could see it now by turning her head sharply to the right. It was yellow and cracked with age, a huge two tunnel affair, that allowed for both the stream and the street to run beneath it. The railroad was still in operation and trains crossed it from time to time both night and day. Now it appeared as a massive stone hulk, with snow above it and streaks of it running across the bridges face. The street side was almost obliterated with snow and she wondered how long it would take for the plows to dig it out.

Her eyes were suddenly drawn to another bridge that crossed the stream almost directly across from her house. A flock of dark colored birds were swooping up and down from it to the stream below. It was the bridge to Anderson College which lay over the hill in a grove of trees about a half mile away. It was a service entrance and not the main one, so that not a lot of traffic entered at that point, but it was the bridge she had crossed nearly every morning for over ten years while teaching there. The walk to work had been one of the joys of her day, and whether it was fall, winter or spring, she had used the twenty minutes to clear her mind and become one with the natural world.

Now the bridge was deep in snow. If she still worked at the college there would be no walking there this morning. And if her beloved husband was still alive there would be no worry over how in the world would the snow on the front walk get shoveled and when and if the awful cloud of depression and anxiety would lift from her. For now, despite the pills she had taken earlier, the cloud descended in a rush. And she leaned hard against the window seat and closed her mind trying to keep the panic at bay.

When she was breathing a bit easier again, she closed the curtains with a shaking hand and headed slowly toward the kitchen. Once there she retrieved the last bottle of wine from the refrigerator and managed to get it open, with the help of a corkscrew which was always left conveniently on the counter. It was a cheap brand of pink Moscato. A sweet wine, it was certainly not her favorite taste, but she had always liked the color of it as she swirled it in her glass and sat in a moment of contemplation. But this morning she poured it directly into the first glass she found in the cupboard above the sink, a large water glass. She poured the wine until it nearly overflowed and then lifted it quickly to her lips. Taking a long swallow of the wine she stumbled to a chair at the kitchen table and sat there trying to keep the thoughts at bay until the wine took effect. There was soon a warmth in her stomach, and her shoulders and abdomen began to relax. Almost at once there was a feeling of nausea and a strange hunger at the same time. Her head throbbed, and she felt as though she was about to pass out. She was hungover, she realized. She hadn't eaten since the day before; she had drunk too much and now this morning she was starting all over again. It was a vicious circle, she realized.

The doctor had prescribed the anxiety and depression medication just after her husbands' death. She had gone to him in a panic, and she remembered his words to her. "It's going to take a while for you to get back on your feet. The medication will help you, but you've got to take it as directed. It will defeat the purpose if you try to adjust the quantities yourself."

She hadn't tried to adjust the quantities. In fact, she had stopped taking it regularly. She hadn't liked the way it made her feel, dark and dismal, nearly like a zombie as she stumbled about the house. She and her husband had often enjoyed a glass of wine in the evening and remembering the warm relaxed feeling it had always left her with, she soon turned to wine and alcohol as her drug of choice. It had worked for a time, but after last night and this morning, she realized if she continued upon this path it would lead to her death. It was a shock to remember the calm happy person she had once been, compared to the pathetic, anxiety ridden alcoholic she had become.

The night before, awaking in the dark as she had with the wind howling and the storm trying to tear the house down, had led her up to a kind of precipice where she had never been before. It would have been so easy to let the fear and panic push her over the edge. Her desperate prayer in the dark had been a true sign to her that she had entered a new phase. There would have to be some changes made, some help if she were to survive. She could call the doctor and make an appointment. She hadn't been to see him for months now. It had been July or maybe August when she had gone back to him. But instead of coming clean with the true way she was feeling, she had simply told him she was doing some better. The look he had given her at the time should have told her he didn't believe her. Doctor Barker had been she and her husband's doctor for longer than she could remember. He had grown old before her eyes, and on that last visit to his office he had reminded her of a weary old man who just wanted to walk away from all the problems he encountered daily.

His face had been drawn and taut and he had nervously fingered his chin as he stared at her. Instead of going over his list of questions as he usually did, he simply told her to make another appointment as she went out, and to continue taking the medication as directed.

Now another glitch had been thrown into the machinery of her daily life. She was trapped in a white world. Her car was trapped in the garage at the back. It hadn't been driven for months. It probably wouldn't start anyway even if she could get to it. Her driveway was blocked in layers of snow, as were the sidewalks. It had never occurred to her that she would have to see to such things. Now that her husband was no longer with her, who would mow the grass, who would shovel the snow? Who would take her hand and lead her through life as he had done for so many years?

Trying to keep tears at bay she slowly got up from the table and moved with care to the counter. She placed a coffee pod in the brewer and waited while the black liquid ran into the mug. When her husband was alive, she had always brewed the largest pot of coffee that she could since he had always consumed three or four cups before going off to work at the fire station. Now it was mug by mug and she had grown used to a new contraption. She found a loaf of bread in the cupboard and dropped two slices into the toaster. She brought butter and strawberry jam from the refrigerator and placed in on the counter. It was odd how the simple task of buttering toast could momentarily take her mind from the current dilemma. Also, quite odd the way she was hungry for the bread and yet repelled by it at the same time, her stomach seeming to be squeezed by queasiness. She placed her toast on a paper plate and carried it and the mug of coffee to the table by the rear window, her hands shaking. Thankfully the curtains were closed, so for a moment she could stare at the table and the coffee and toast before her. At least the orange Fiesta mug was pleasant to the eye, and the wisps of steam rising from the cup led her to lift the mug as best as she could to take a long swallow. For a moment she thought her stomach would reject the strong liquid, but it soon settled, and she took another sip. She finally lifted a slice of toast to her mouth, the scent of the strawberry jam awakening her taste buds, when the front doorbell rang.

The sudden metallic sound of the bell echoed through the house and rattled her equilibrium, causing her to drop the toast she had lifted, unleashing crumbs to scatter across the white surface of the cloth. It had been days since the bell had rang; the last time a couple of elders from the Mormon church had tried introducing her to their organization. She had nearly closed the door in their faces. Now it was early morning and her world was encapsulated in snow. Who could possibly want anything from her at a time like this? She suddenly found herself unable to move, nearly paralyzed by fear. She would just sit still and wait until whoever was outside realized no one would be answering the door this morning.

But after a couple moments of silence the doorbell rang again seemingly louder than before. The shrill sound brought her back to life and brought her weakly to her feet. Nearly forced by fear, she moved slowly through the hall to the front door. She stood there breathing hard, and, fingers shaking, pushed the small curtain aside. Her right hand was drawn to her chest in surprise when she saw who was standing knee deep in snow, staring back at the window.

CHAPTER 2

I t was a young boy who stood there with a snow
shovel in his hand. As far as she could remember she
had never seen him before. He appeared to be around
twelve years old, wearing a thin looking jacket, a bit
inappropriate for the weather, and a blue ski cap from
which his longish hair surrounded his head and pale
face. Kath detected a bit of shivering as he stood there
waiting for the door to be answered. His eyes were
wide, and his breath appeared frosty on the morning
air. At least he wore gloves, though they seemed over
large and quite dirty.

Despite her anxiety and trepidation, Kath quickly
opened the door, her hands shaking a bit, as the cold
air hit her in the face. It was a shock to her already sensitized system.

"Do you need someone to shovel your snow," the
boy spoke, his voice high pitched against the sound
of the wind which still whipped snow from the trees
across the street. "I can do it for you cheap."

"Why yes, if you would like," Kath spoke, after a
moment, relief in her voice. It was nearly a shock to her
that only a few moments before she was in a bit of despair, not knowing how she could ever get dug out from
the storm. And then as though summoned by a power
beyond herself, this good Samaritan had appeared,

shovel in hand to do her bidding. "And who are you," she went on, about to be driven inside by the cold and her own anxiety. "I'm Mrs. Longley."

"My name's Marcus Warner," the boy answered.

"I've never seen you before. Do you live around here?"

"Yes, up there at the end of Park Street, right where it turns and goes under the railroad."

"Oh, up there by the tunnel."

"Yes, right there."

Kath knew exactly where he lived. There were three or four mobile homes in a row right below the railroad embankment. She and her husband had often gone by them on an evening walk around the neighborhood. Park Street entered a short tunnel there that led under the railroad, and suddenly became Mountain View Avenue as it led away into the upper valley. The trailers were rundown and overgrown, and she had often wondered about the folks who must live there. Now one of the residents stood before her, still shivering.

"You'd best get started," she said then. "It's freezing out here. Just start with the sidewalks in front and to the side. There's the driveway also, but it doesn't need done right away. You can come back tomorrow or whenever you can. If you get too cold you can come inside later to warm up. Okay?"

The boy, Marcus, looked at her strangely, his eyes wide, and nodded his head. He turned quickly and began to scrape at the snow at the edge of the porch. She stood for a few seconds and watched his progress. Now, he appeared to be a well-oiled machine, energetic and determined, despite the cold. He would probably play out in time, but it would be interesting to find out just how much he could accomplish.

Kath went back inside and closed the door. She stood just inside for a moment catching her breath. What an extraordinary stroke of luck that this stranger had appeared seemingly from nowhere. It was surprising how much of a weight had been lifted from her mind that threatened at any moment to break.

She went back to the kitchen, and before sitting down again at the table, she recorked the bottle of wine she had opened earlier and put it back into the refrigerator. She threw away the cold toast and poured the remaining coffee into the sink. Then she popped another pod into the brewer and once the coffee was hot in the mug again, she added cream and sweetener and sat down at the table. Finally, she put some fresh bread into the toaster.

It was strange, she thought, sitting there sipping at the coffee, how answering the door and talking to the boy for a few moments had caused her to momentarily forget her anxiety and feeling of desperation. The book she had been reading about anxiety and its causes and cures, had spent several pages explaining how occupation could play a large role in an anxiety sufferer getting well again. How allowing oneself to become involved with a hobby or interacting with another person could help to move one along a track that would eventually lead to relief.

In any case, at this moment, she came to a sudden decision that for this one day at least she would not touch another drop of wine. It had helped her at the most desperate moments to hold herself together, but as time had passed it had left her, as it had this morning, with an awful hangover that only helped to increase the sense of impending death, or at the very least, a desperate sense of falling apart. The pills she had taken earlier had given her some relief without the worst of the side effects. After the night of terror she had experienced, she would hold on to a thread of hope, that by following the doctors instructions she could at least be able to go through the motions of living. She would probably find herself craving the taste of the wine before days end. So many nights had been faced with a glass in her hand. But what she couldn't face was a night like the one that just been passed, a dark desperate night of fear, desperation and panic.

A few moments later after sipping some more coffee and slowly eating a couple of pieces of buttered toast, which calmed the queasy feeling in her stomach, she went to the side window in the living room to see how much progress Marcus was making. Surprisingly, he was nearly to the end of her property line, and she watched as he carefully removed shovel after shovel of the nearly a foot of snow that had fallen. Due to the drifting from the wind of the night before it came nearly to his waist at places. But it didn't seem to be a heavy snow by the ease with which he worked. At one point she saw him stop and move his eyes from side to side to see that he had reached the end of her walk. He was about to turn and come back when she saw a man emerge from the house that sat just beyond her drive. It was Harvey Kline, her neighbor. He was dressed for the weather in a dark overcoat and a fur hat. He had a perpetual mean look on his face and stood glaring at Marcus who had turned by this time and was walking back along the walk he had just cleared.

Mr. Kline said nothing, but Marcus must have heard him emerge from the house, for he turned for a few seconds to see who it was, then continued coming back toward the house. Kath turned from the window and went back to the kitchen. Sitting down again at the table, she couldn't get Harvey Kline off her mind. He had lived next door even before Kath and her husband moved to Bridgetown. He was a bachelor and a loner. He was also a nasty troublemaker, always gossiping and complaining. It was her husband who finally befriended him after a series of domestic disputes about property lines and the proper disposal of leaf and grass clippings. Then for years he and her husband had gotten along splendidly. Her husband could do no wrong in Harvey Kline's eyes. But when it came to her there were no smiles or kind words. It was as though she didn't exist, and Kath had concluded that he hated women. Did he have a secret longing for men? She had often questioned her husband as to how he had tamed the savage beast. The answer he gave was always the same. "Because I understood him. He's lonely and scared. He thinks everyone is his enemy. He's a bit mental and suffers from OCD. By talking to him and questioning his feelings I was able to bring him out of his shell. He has grown to trust me."

Kline and her husband had been friendly neighbors until the day Fred died. After that however, it was business as usual. He had not attended Fred's funeral, nor had he offered her a word of sympathy or a bit of help of any kind. In fact, his obvious dislike of her had increased over the past few months. Any stick or stone, leaf or grass clipping that ended up on his driveway which was only a few feet from hers would end up on her side. It was as though he were baiting her, egging her on to a fight. Up to this point she had avoided any conflict, although she had wanted at times to lash out at him in some way, as she had the day just after the funeral when she sat on her back patio in the deepest possible despair. Her husband was gone, and her life was finished. Kline had walked up his driveway until he was just opposite her and stopped. Out of the corner of her eye she saw him and turned thinking he was going to walk toward her or at least speak to her with a comforting word. Instead he stood there and glared at her, a look of pure hate on his face.

She had broken into tears then. What could she possibly have done to make him dislike her so much? Did he blame her for Fred's death? Had some other woman, girl friend or mother, wounded him in the past so that he was transferring his hatred to her? She knew at that moment, as she did this morning, that one day she would have to face him and let him know how terrible his behavior toward her had been and how much pain it had caused her.

She was still sitting at the table musing when the doorbell rang again. Only this time she wasn't quite as startled, and she went quickly to the front door and opened it. Marcus stood there, shovel in hand, breathing hard. His face was quite red from the cold and his hands were shaking.

"I finished the sidewalk," he said. Is there anything else you want me to shovel?"

"Yes, there is more," she told him. "But you must be freezing. Why don't you come in for a few moments and get warm again?"

The boy seemed to hesitate for a moment, moving

his eyes from side to side as though he wasn't sure how to react.

"Come on inside," she insisted. "Once you're warm again you can shovel some more if you like."

He hesitated for a moment and then nodded his head. His boots were covered with snow and he stamped them hard on the mat before coming into the house. Kath stepped aside, and Marcus entered the hallway. For the first time in a while Kath looked around her and saw how unkempt and sad looking the house had become since Fred's death. She hadn't run the vacuum cleaner or lifted a broom in a long time. As she was closing the door, she heard a snowplow in the distance, rumbling slowly toward her. By the end of the day she at least would lose some of her panic over being snowed in and trapped.

"Would you like something to drink," Kath asked, as she moved slowly toward the kitchen, Marcus following her, seeming to take small steps as though he had entered a forbidden place, while looking all around him, wide eyed.

"I can give you hot chocolate," she told him as they entered the kitchen. I think there may be some coke in the refrigerator and of course I have plenty of water."

She pulled out a chair for him at the table and he gingerly sat down. Close-up, his eyes seemed to have a frightened look and the skin of his face was pale and patchy. Was it a look of hunger, she wondered, or one of fear as though he didn't quite understand her bit of kindness?

"Would you like some hot chocolate," she asked, once Marcus was settled and breathing easier now that he was out of the cold.

"I could drink some coffee," he said finally, obviously noticing the mug on the table which was still half full of her own drink.

Do you like coffee," she asked. "Do you really drink it? The chocolate..." She was going to say might be better for you, but his voice stopped her.

"No, I drink coffee all the time," he said. "It's good with sugar and milk..."

Kath went quickly to the brewer and popped a pod inside, taking a mug from the cupboard. She chose a light blue one since that color always gave her a sense of peace and calmness, although lately no simple colored mug could do anything for her. Perhaps it would help her young visitor to feel more at home.

It took only a couple of minutes for the coffee to be fixed and she carried the steaming mug to the table along with a carton of milk and some handy sugar packets and sat it in front of him.

"You can put as much milk and sugar in as you would like," she told him.

But Marcus sat there for a moment staring at the mug and then toward the counter where the coffee brewer sat.

"How did you make that so fast," he asked, a curious tone in his voice.

"It's the brewer. The coffee comes in pods," she answered. "It's fast and convenient. Haven't you seen one before?"

Yes, I've seen them," he said quickly, as though wanting to sound more knowledgeable. "But we don't have one at home. My mother makes it on the stove in a coffee pot..."

He was silent then and began fixing his coffee,

pouring the milk with a slightly shaking hand. A few drops landed on the table top, and a grimace crossed his face, as though he expected her to yell at him. Kath quickly took a paper napkin, reached across the table and wiped up the spill. Marcus relaxed.

"How old are you, Marcus," Kath asked once she was settled at the table and the boy had had his first long swallow of coffee.

"I'm thirteen," he answered. "I'll be fourteen in July."

"And you live with just your parents, or do you have brothers or sisters?"

"No, just my parents and me."

"I've never seen you around. But then there are a lot of young people in the neighborhood. I guess I haven't noticed."

"I don't get away from the house much...," he said, and then stopped himself, as though afraid to say more.

"You go to school, don't you?" Kath asked. "What grade are you in?"

"I did go to school, but I stopped going when I was in fifth grade."

"Stopped going? Why in the world..."

"I'm home schooled," he said quickly. "I was bullied, and my grades were bad..."

He clammed up then and Kath was afraid to question him further. It was obvious he didn't want to discuss his situation any longer. But she noticed by the look on his face that there was a lot he was hiding, and that he seemed troubled in some way.

They sat silently at the table until Marcus had finished his coffee. Kath offered him some chocolate chip cookies she had found in the cupboard, but he shook his head. There was a look of hunger in his eyes as though he wanted to eat them, but he quickly stood up.

"I better get back to my shoveling," he said. "You said you had more..."

"Yes, you can do the patio in the back," She told him. "And perhaps the walk back to the shed. We won't worry about the driveway. I haven't taken the car out for weeks. It probably won't even start. Anyway, the driveway can be difficult. If I decide to have it done later, I'll let you know. Besides, my neighbor can be a bit of a problem anyway. If one flake of snow from my driveway went over to his he would scream bloody murder."

"Yes, I know," Marcus suddenly spoke, "He yelled at me!"

"He yelled at you? When, this morning?"

"Yeah..."

Kath was suddenly curious. She had seen Kline from the window, but as far as she could tell he hadn't spoken a word.

"What did he say to you," she asked. "I looked out the window and saw him come out of the house. But it didn't look like he spoke. Did he come out earlier?"

"No, I... I don't think so..." Marcus seemed suddenly confused. His face turned a bit red. "Maybe I just thought he yelled. It's windy..." He stopped then and headed toward the door. Kath followed and as he opened it to go out, Kath suddenly realized how thin he looked. The bulky coat had made him appear a bit larger, but his legs were oddly shaped and didn't quite fill the faded jeans he wore, wet now from all the traipsing in the snow. Earlier she had noticed he wore a dirty tee shirt under the coat.

After giving him instructions for clearing the back walk and the patio, he went out again and she closed the door. Kath stood there for a moment, her hand on the door knob, her mind beginning to race. The wind still whistled a bit and the sound of the snow plow was louder. While Kath knew Kline, next door, was certainly capable of yelling, silence was his game with her. So why in the world would he yell at Marcus when he hadn't even crossed her own driveway? And then turning weakly to head back to the kitchen, she was even more curious to know if the boy had deliberately lied about Kline's yelling at him.

And why would that even bother me, she thought as she sat down again at the table. All young people with over active imaginations lied. She was sure she had lied a bit growing up. And caught in one she was sure her mother, being the kind understanding woman she had been, would just have smiled and brushed the whole thing aside with a tap on the shoulder or a hug. It was only big lies, she would have reminded her, the ones that involved other people and hurt them in some way that mattered.

She was still sitting there musing an hour later when a knock came to the back door. When she got up from the table and opened it, she found Marcus standing there looking quite exhausted. The patio was clear, she noticed, and the walk to the shed had been uncovered.

"Well I'm finished," he said. "Unless you have something more for me to do, I'd better get going. My parents will be wondering what happened to me."

"Step in for a moment and I'll get you some money," Kath said. "How much do you charge."

"Just give me ten dollars."

"Ten dollars? That's not enough, not for all the work you've done." She stood there for a moment not sure of where she had put her purse the night before. Then she remembered she had shoved it under the sofa as she did so many times at night when she's been drinking. The thought of wine suddenly had her desiring a drink. Her anxiety was rising, and a feeling of panic was closing in. She found the purse, grabbed some bills and when she got back to the kitchen Marcus was still standing like a statue by the back door. The look on his face was suddenly like that of a scared deer, and he kept staring out the window as though he needed to be away fast.

"Here's fifty dollars," Kath said nervously as she peeled the bills in her hand. Will that be enough?"

"That's too much," he protested. "I can't take that much!"

"You can, and you will," Kath insisted. "You were like an angel to me this morning. What would I have done if you hadn't come along? Why in the world did you come here to me first anyway? There's lots of other houses along Bridge Street."

"This is the first house I saw when I came down Park Street."

"Mr. Gordon's house is closer. Across from me on the hill."

"Someone was already shoveling up there," He said, looking down at his feet. "I didn't know if you needed someone to shovel, but I stopped to ask anyway."

"Well I'm glad you did. You will never know how happy I am that you stopped here." She reached out and took his hand and folded the money into it. Marcus took it gingerly, looking at the bills as though to be sure they were real.

What will you so with the money," Kath asked, "save it or spend it?"

"I'll keep it until I get enough to buy a new pair of shoes." He shoved the bills into his coat pocket and opened the door. "Thanks," he said at last. "I'd better be going."

And he was gone almost as quickly as he had arrived. A silence settled over the house then, almost deeper and depressing than before. Kath trudged into the living room and a strange feeling of exhaustion settled over her. She sank for a moment into her Lazy Boy chair. She was tired and almost too worn out for any anxiety to gain a foothold into her thoughts. And there were many things to be thought of.

Marcus was certainly a curious boy. It was very strange how he had shown up that morning. She had spoken to very few people in the weeks that had passed since her husband died. Now it seemed her life as a hermit, as an agoraphobic alcoholic had been interrupted. Or perhaps it had served a purpose and was ending. The short conversation she had had with this strange boy was the first one she had had with anyone in a long time. For years Fred had been her best friend, and they had spent so much time together. There were a few couples they did things with, but after his death she had been a third wheel and it was as though she were now a stranger. Perhaps it was just that very few people knew what to say to a grieving widow.

It was strange that while her mind was on the young visitor earlier, she had momentarily forgotten her own fear and terror. And then it came back to her quite sharply. During the height of her panic the night before she had wanted to die. She had called out to the universe for help, to give her something to live for, a reason to go on. Was this strange boy, this good Samaritan who had appeared at her door this morning, a thread to lead her to the peace she longed for?

CHAPTER 3

S omehow, despite her distress, Kath fell asleep. Her dreams were filled with anxiety. In one of them she was on top of a hill with a sled looking down. The bottom was obscured by fog. Her husband, Fred, was there with her. He also had a sled, and he got onto his and called to her to follow. But she was afraid and for a moment she stood frozen to the spot. What lay below her, trees, a cliff? Somehow, against her better judgement, she got onto the sled and pushed off down the hill. She shut her eyes tight and help her breath as the sled plunged downhill at a dizzying pace. And then suddenly the sled came to a stop and she opened her eyes. She was sitting in a peaceful glade in the woods. All around her the evergreen trees were tufted with snow and the sun was shining through the clouds. Her husband was gone but she was filled with a sense of peace and joy, and she was breathing deeply with relief.

It was the last dream she remembered upon waking up. What in the world had it meant? Did Fred want her to follow him into the peaceful world she had glimpsed? Or was it a sign that she would eventually come back from the world of fear and anxiety she currently inhabited? The peaceful feeling the dream had left her with lasted for only a few moments and then she could feel the anxiety seep into her arms and her back, then into her brain where it uncovered her desire for alcohol. She thought of the bottle of wine in the refrigerator and wanted to get out of the chair at once and retrieve it, along with a glass from the cupboard. But remembering her promise to herself she stayed where she was and pulled an afghan up around her neck.

The room seemed suddenly chilly and she looked around at her surroundings. The TV sat silently on a stand in front of her. She had always enjoyed turning it on and watching a movie or a news program. The list of her television interests was endless. But the set hadn't been turned on in days. The wall near her chair held a wide bookcase filled with her favorite books. She hadn't gone near it in weeks. One book lay on a stand near her chair. A novel, it was the latest by one of her favorite writers. She couldn't remember when she had last picked it up, or what it was even about, and it was beginning to gather dust. Her husband's chair, just beyond the stand seemed emptier today than it ever had. Now it was inhabited by Fred's neatly folded afghan. Brown and a bit shabby and worn, it had been like a child's security blanket to him, and now she wished she had wrapped it around him as he lay in his coffin.

Tears welled up in her eyes and she began to weep. How many times had she rolled into a ball to cry since Fred's death? She certainly was no stranger to tears, but no matter how many she had shed or how often she had wailed against the world, he was still gone, and she was still very much alone. After a moment, she pulled herself together. A feeling of extreme hunger swept over her and she gathered strength to get out of the chair. The light in the room had changed. Was it already afternoon? From outside came the sound of cars passing along the street in front of the house. Obviously, the snow plows had finished their work.

In the kitchen finally, the wall clock told her it was nearly four o'clock. She had slept for a long time. But sleep had been needed. Sleep was a good escape. The desire for a drink, the need for a pill nearly consumed her, but instead she opened the refrigerator and took out bacon and eggs. Her hands shook a bit as she prepared the food. And even though the smell of the bacon cooking somehow made her feel a bit nauseous, when everything was prepared, she managed sit at the table and eat some of it. It seemed to her that it had very little taste, but at least she was eating something and gradually her stomach began to calm again. It will take some time, she thought when her meal was finished, and she was sitting there wondering what the next step would be. Words formed in her head and it was as though Fred were there with her, on the other side of the table where he usually sat, speaking to her, "Time will take care of things; this too, will pass."

She made it through the night by taking her pills and overcoming her desire for alcohol. At times it was hard. Her hand would reach for a glass or she would turn toward the refrigerator wanting to pull out the bottle she had uncorked earlier in the day. If left there the wine would sour, become stale. The desire caught her and nearly held her, but she remained strong.

When she awoke the next morning, it was without the extreme panic of the day before. Sunlight poured through the windows and seemed to write lines of brightness on the walls of the room. She was still exhausted, and her muscles ached, but the panic had pulled back like an army, yet still surrounded her at a distance. Here in the circle of safety she inhabited she could at least have some semblance of a life. She got up from the bed and got ready for the day. Dressed in slacks and a warm sweater she stood at the top of the stairs and realized that her surroundings had somehow come into a sharper focus. Suddenly past habits came back to her in a rush. Before Fred died, she had gone first thing each morning into her "office", the smallest of the four upstairs rooms. She had fashioned it into her own personal space, with a desk and a chair, a bookcase, a more comfortable chair for lounging and a small table. It was here that she had always sat and planned her days. Personal lists were made, and her mounds of career materials were gone through. Her desk sat in front of a wide window through which she could observe the outside world, the weather, nature and its seasonal colors and changes. She would often open the window, if the temperature was right, and feel the breeze with its rhythms and scents touch her face and bring her to life.

Suddenly the space beckoned. She turned from the stairs and stood staring at the door to the room. Why did it seem like a forbidden world to her suddenly? She could not go inside. It seemed in her sensitized mind that something was waiting inside that she didn't want to face. And then she realized she had gone through the door the morning Fred died. The telephone was there, and she had called 911. But now it was nearly a year later, and she could count on one hand the number of times she had been inside the room since then.

Now she took a deep breath, turned the knob, opened the door and stepped inside. The light through the window was the first thing she noticed. The window faced Bridge Street and even from the doorway the trees on the other side of the stream were visible. The atmosphere of the room took a moment to settle around her. It smelled the same, but a scent of staleness seemed to have invaded the place. She moved to the desk and sat down in the chair for a moment. Her journal still lay to the left on the desk. Black and ominous looking, it still lay open to the last entry she had written, May 29, 2017, the day before her husbands' death. She reached to close it, but suddenly pulled her shaking hand back. She had once found joy and comfort in writing in her journal. Each morning she had done so before anything else, just a line or two or perhaps a whole paragraph of how the day had been spent. What was the weather like and what were her plans for the day ahead? Remembering those days brought some peace to her heart. She would write again soon, she promised herself.

It was here at her desk that she always planned her day of teaching at the college. How she had loved that job. Stacked neatly on the right side of the desk was the day book she had kept, and a few of the notebooks and lesson planners she had saved. It was all behind her now, but besides the pleasant memories she had kept of her students and the few professors she had worked along side of, inside her there was a deep sense of anger, almost hatred of Robert Sterner, for the way he had behaved toward her, for how he had caused her so much pain and anguish, so much sadness. If Fred had lived, he could have helped her make a much smoother transition into retirement. But when he died, and she had had to add another layer of grief to an already overloaded mind, the anger and disappointment over how her career had ended, festered and seethed inside her. Someday she realized she would have to find a way to release it. Obviously, it was contributing quite a lot to the anxiety state she currently found herself lost in.

She sat down at the desk, found a comfortable position in the chair, and pulled out the top drawer of the desk. Inside, lay a large pad, and there was a wide slot filled with pencils and pens. She lifted the pad out along with a pen that had once been a favorite. In the past she had always sat there for a few moments and made lists of things she wanted to accomplish that day. Since the room had stayed shut after Fred's death, she had used the kitchen table as a desk and one of the drawers at the counter to hold pads pencils and checkbook. She had kept up with the household bills and paid other necessary ones, but she no longer kept lists. It had been too hard for her to accomplish even the simplest chores, and looking beyond the moment had been quite difficult, but now she was sitting at her desk again and the blank pad that lay in front of her seemed to demand attention.

She picked up the pen in a shaking hand and wrote, Get me out of here. The desire to get up from the chair and go running down the stairs was overwhelming. But she closed her eyes and took a deep breath and stayed seated in the chair. What should she write? She began by writing a list of necessary things she should call into the market for delivery. Simple things, basic things, what did it matter if she already had some of it stashed away somewhere? She did manage to write down slowly, a list of things that would help her survive the next few days. She couldn't even remember the day or the date, but after a moment of wracking her brain, she realized it was a weekday, Wednesday, Thursday? The last time she had turned on the TV was the previous Sunday for they had been going on and on about the impending blizzard that would probably hit in the middle of the week.

She drew a dark line across the center of the pad just then and shaking her head she wrote, go to see Doctor Barker. When she took her pill earlier, she had seen on the label that there were no refills left. She would have to find a way to get to his office, but how? It was located in a medical facility at least three miles away. Her car was snowed in inside the garage. It probably wouldn't even start. And if she did get it running, she was already anticipating the incredible feat it would be for her to drive herself there. The anxiety she would face would be incredible...

It was as though the whole fabric of her life was an impossible maze from which she would never find a way out of. She was about to lay down her pen in defeat and get up from the chair when the doorbell sounded from downstairs. She was startled a bit at hearing the sound, but she rose quickly and left the room, as calmly as she could, and made her way down the stairs and directly to the front door.

Panic rose in her as her shaking hand reached out for the door knob. Opening the door, she was relieved to find Marcus standing there with his shovel. He was dressed as he had been the day before, in the same rough looking coat and hat, the same faded jeans and oversized boots. This time he smiled when she opened the door and she smiled back. It was comforting to see him standing there and it was hard to believe she had only met him yesterday.

"Marcus," she said, "I wasn't expecting you this soon. Leave your shovel there and come in and have a cup of coffee with me."

"I thought I might start to shovel your driveway this morning," he said quickly. "It's not quite as cold as yesterday."

"Yes, you can if you're sure you want to," she said. "But first come in and warm up a bit before you start. I'll make you some coffee."

He stepped inside without hesitation, after stomping hard on the mat to clear them of any traces of snow.

"Don't worry about your feet," she said, closing the door, "It can easily be wiped up."

In the kitchen she insisted he remove his coat before sitting down at the table. At first, he shook his head, but Kath insisted, and he removed it at last, revealing a ragged looking tee shirt that had seen better days. It was printed with an image of what looked like a dog, but the animal was unrecognizable after so much wear. Marcus's arms were remarkably thin, and there was a bruise on one of them, just below the sleeve, an ugly discolored mark that seemed to surround the entire limb.

"What happened to your arm," she asked when he had finally sat down, and she was about to turn to the coffee maker. "I hope you didn't get that from all the shoveling you did for me yesterday."

"Oh no," he answered quickly. "I banged up against our house when I was shoveling there yesterday. There was a lot of ice and I slipped..."

It seemed to her as though he wanted to say more,

but he turned his face to the window suddenly, the sunlight revealing the fact that he may not have been telling the truth about how he got the bruise.

Kath quickly made him coffee in a mug her husband had often used, one with a picture of a bright red fire truck wrapped around the surface of it. She placed it along with sugar and creamer on the table in front of him. His hands shook a bit as he carefully poured the cream and spooned the sugar.

As he took a sip of the coffee Kath noticed him take a rather long glance at the firetruck on the mug. He looked at her, a bit inquisitively.

"It was my husband's mug," she said, finally sitting down opposite him with her own coffee. "He was a fireman.

"Where is he..."

"He died last year," Kath stirred her coffee. "It was sudden. A heart attack."

"I'm sorry," Marcus stammered, lowering his eyes. "I wondered if you were married..."

Yes, I was married for many years. It's been nearly a year since Fred died."

"Did you have any...kids?"

"No. I couldn't have any. There was just Fred and me. We thought for a couple of years of adopting but time passed, and we grew used to being alone together."

Kath stopped herself. This boy was really a stranger to her. She shouldn't be revealing her personal history to him. Who was he anyway, and could he be trusted? She suddenly turned the tables and focused on Marcus.

"Do you mind not going to school," she asked? "I mean did you ever go to public school?"

"I did go..." he answered, after thinking for a

moment. "But when I went to Middle School, I had to ride the bus and the boys beat up on me...They picked at me because my clothes were old, and they said I looked funny...My mother decided I should be home schooled since I was getting into a lot of fights."

"Have you been keeping up? I mean are you where you need to be?"

"My mother takes care of all of that..."

"What grade are you in, or would be in if you went to school?"

"I think seventh..."

"You think."

Marcus threw her a strange look and dropped his eyes. Kath suddenly realized she had entered a world where she didn't belong. The boy in front of her was here to shovel her driveway, not to be questioned or grilled.

Suddenly feeling a bit hungry Kath suddenly thought that food might be a safer subject to discuss with the boy. "I'm about to fix myself some breakfast," she said. "Are you hungry? Can I fix you something?"

"No, I already ate cereal before I came." Marcus said firmly. He took a last drink of his coffee and emptied the mug. "I'd better get started with the shoveling."

When he had put on his coat again, and headed toward the front door, Kath found her own winter coat in the hall closet and accompanied him outside to the front porch. The shock of the bright, blinding sunlight and the chilly air stopped her for a moment, and she held onto the bannister and caught her breath. It was as though she were suddenly a fish out of water and it was very hard for her to breathe. She felt the anxiety begin to descend and she closed her eyes trying to keep it at bay. It was like this lately whenever she attempted to move outside the safety of her own four walls.

"Are you okay?" Marcus asked from the steps in front of her.

"Oh, I'm fine," she said, pulling herself together. "It's just a shock to come out into the cold…"

For a moment she focused on the street in front of her. A car passed, birds rose and fell over the stream opposite. Marcus moved to the sidewalk and Kath followed him, shivering wildly. They stopped where the sidewalk met the drive.

"Be careful where you throw the snow," she told him, her voice weak in the frosty air. Always throw it to my side, otherwise old man Kline will throw a fit. I don't want him yelling at you and believe me he will if you stray one inch over the line. But remember I have about three feet beyond my drive, so you'll be safe."

Marcus went right to work, pushing his shovel into the wall of snow and sending a mound of it flying in the direction of the house. It surprised her that a boy of his size and weight could be so strong. Kath, feeling quite vulnerable from the cold and the wall of anxiety surrounding her, turned and hurried back toward the safety of the house. Once inside, she stood leaning against the door. The feeling of sensitization was stronger than ever. And that is what the book had called it. She even knew what had caused it, the two major life changing events that happened barely a year apart, her retirement and Fred's death. But knowing the cause of her anguish didn't suddenly eradicate it. That would take time, the doctor who wrote the book had said, but eventually, somewhat like a broken leg, her condition would heal. That thought caused her to shake her head and open her eyes. A few days before she would have rushed to her bottle of wine for comfort. And it was not that the desire was not strong in her. She could nearly taste it, smell it, and feel that momentarily relief as it numbed her, caused the very air around her to put her into a bubble of protection.

The pill she had taken earlier did seem to be working a bit of magic. There was some reality to her thoughts. Layer by layer the anxiety was lifting so that she was able to clear the sink of the few dirty dishes and then pull the vacuum sweeper from the hall closet and began cleaning the hallway. It had been months since she had done a thorough cleaning of the house, so she would do what she could and room by room and space by space, she would be able to finish the job. She had completed the kitchen and dining room when she heard, over the hum of the cleaner, a sound of hard knocking on the kitchen door.

She quickly shut of the machine and hurried to the kitchen. Opening the door, she found Marcus in some distress. His face was red, and his hands were shaking.

"What is it, Marcus, what's wrong?"

"That old man is out in his driveway and he yelled at me."

"What did he say?"

"He said I shoveled snow on his drive, but I didn't Mrs. Longley!"

"Did he go back inside or is he still out there?"

"He's still there and he follows along as I shovel, watching me!"

"You go back out and I'll come out and take care of this!"

Kath found her coat and quickly hurried outside.

Kline was indeed standing in his own driveway dressed in a black wool coat and hat. His face was sharp and cold, and his frosty breath reminded her of an angry dragon about to breathe fire.

"What seems to be the problem, Mr. Kline," she asked, trying to keep her voice strong and steady. She half expected at the sound of her voice that he would retreat into his own house. It had been months since he spoken a word to her. Why would he break his silence now?

"This kid is shoveling snow onto my property," Kline yelled, his voice as high and whiney as she remembered. Though when he spoke to Fred it had always been much lower and softer.

"I didn't do that," Mrs. Longley," Marcus said in protest. "Not even one shovelful. I did what you told me and shoveled toward your side of the drive."

Kath quickly surveyed the driveway. Marcus was nearly halfway to the garage and she could see the even line of snow he had removed, piled as neatly as possible on her own property as he went. Then she glanced at Kline's driveway and saw not the slightest bit of snow that Marcus might have put there.

Anger rose in her, for what she saw was an old troublemaker just trying to stir things up. He had not done one thing to be neighborly, or even shown even the slightest bit of kindness or sympathy when Fred died. She had had enough.

"I don't see any snow on your driveway," Kath said angrily. "The boy said he didn't shovel toward you and I believe him!"

"Indeed, he did!" Kline yelled. "I saw him with my own eyes."

"Well maybe you should have your eyes checked," Kath countered. "Obviously you're imagining things!"

Kline suddenly stood up straight, anger in the very air around him. "Why I never! I'll do something about this. I'll go..."

"Do what you will, and go where you must," Kath said loudly. "But this boy is working for me. Leave him alone! And I suggest if you want to avoid any real action on my part, you try being a decent neighbor to me for once, just as you were toward Fred!"

Kath turned toward Marcus who had retreated to the very edge of the driveway. She laid her hand on his shoulder, realizing by the hurt look on the boy's face that the encounter with her neighbor had spooked hm a bit.

Don't worry about him Marcus." She said. "He's just a troublemaker and is looking for attention." She said it loudly enough for Kline to hear, but when she looked toward the spot where he had been standing, it was empty. Her neighbor had obviously slunk back inside. She was sure that her words had stung him. He had obviously thought she would say nothing since there had been such a long silence between them. She was not a person to ever let anger get the better of her. Fred had often told her she was too nice, and that people took advantage of her. "Sometimes you have to fight back and defend yourself. Otherwise you let them have the control they crave!"

Going back inside she thought of his words. She fixed another mug of coffee and sat back down at the table. The feeling of anger inside her was palpable. She could hardly believe she had stood up to Kline in the driveway. She thought of her mother who had instilled the idea in her that it was best to walk away from a fight or even an argument. And her mother had had a rather sad life, she realized. Her father had been hard on her and dominated her every move. She had never done anything in life without his approval and as a result had never done one thing that brought her happiness. Fred had never been that way with her. He had encouraged her since the early years of their marriage to have friends and outside interests. He had never encouraged her to have anger or bad feelings toward another person, but he had often told her to stand up and be seen. Never hide from your enemy. And yet she had never thought of Kline as her enemy. She had simply thought of him as an old man who was cranky and ill natured. His reasons for hating women as he obviously did were buried inside of himself and were no concern of hers.

Kath realized how wrong she had been about that thought an hour later when Marcus came once again to the door and knocked loudly, bringing her out of her reverie. He was breathing hard and seemed bothered about something.

"I didn't quite get to the garage yet," he said excitedly. "But I did shovel a path the rest of the way, and there's a big pile of tree limbs behind it and lots of leaves. I couldn't get around it."

Kath stood there puzzled. She had never used the back of her garage for a dumping ground. Fred had always kept the back of their property neat and well groomed. She put her coat on again and went out with Marcus to the driveway. He still had a way to go, but the pathway he had shoveled up to the garage and along one side of the building, allowed her to see the pile of debris that had been placed there. And someone had put it there, she realized. The wind had not blown it there nor had it fallen from the sky in a freakish twist of nature. It was Kline who had done it, and obviously had done it the previous fall. She had not noticed, no doubt, because she was inside the house, lounging around in an alcoholic stupor.

Kath glanced across at Kline's property. A large maple tree looked as so some of its lower limbs were missing. Obviously, her neighbor had done some major pruning. She turned her attention to his house where at one of the back windows a curtain fell back into place. Kline had been watching and knew now, she was sure, that his invasion of her property had been discovered.

Kath stood there shaking a bit, from the cold or from her anger and anxiety, she couldn't be sure. She wanted to flee in panic, but she stood her ground. "We won't worry about this now," she said to Marcus. "Just work on the driveway so I can get to the car. We'll deal with this later."

Back at the house she shook her head at the brazen audacity of her neighbor. He had blown his top over an imaginary bit of snow he claimed had been thrown at his own driveway, knowing that he had dumped piles of his litter behind her garage. She felt as though she should go to his front door and bang on it until he opened it, and then she could scream at him and let him know how much she had been hurt by his behavior. But no, that would be like getting even and going against everything she believed in. But there was a better way of defending herself. She had suggested it to Fred long ago when they had first realized how Kline operated. And as soon as she was back on her feet, a bit more than she was today, she would put her plan into action, and then Kline would know she was through with his hatefulness and bad behavior!

CHAPTER 4

Later that night as she lay in bed trying to sleep, Kath went over and over in her mind trying to come up with the lines one of her favorite poets, Robert Frost, had written about fences and good neighbors. She had read the entire poem to Fred before suggesting they build a fence between their driveway and Kline's property. Perhaps that would stop the trouble he had started to give them, the pettiness of his daily rants. Of course, Fred had said he didn't think it was a good idea, but mostly because the cost, even at that time, would have put a large hole in their savings.

She gave up on finding in her crowded mind the lines of the poem, but she knew that as soon as spring came, and she was a lot stronger, the fence would be built, and not just between the driveways but all around the back of her property. Kline would never again throw anything on her land, unless he threw it over the fence. She would order the highest wooden fence they had. Money was no object now. She and Fred had been very good about saving for a rainy day, and, she still received a decent retirement income.

Marcus had finished shoveling the driveway around noon that day with no more interference from Kline. When he came to the door and told her he was finished, he had had a look of triumph on his face and she had gone out with him at once. The door was automatic, but she had not opened it for so long she couldn't remember where she had placed the remote. After trudging back to the house and finding it in her purse along with her car keys, she was able to go back outside and open the door. Her car, an eight-year-old white Toyota, sat there looking dirty and dinghy in the glaring winter light. With Marcus looking on expectantly, she crawled into the car and with a shaking hand placed the key in the ignition. But when she turned it nothing happened. She tried again and again but still the engine did not turn over. She crawled back out of the car in defeat. But she really hadn't expected it to start and there was nothing more she could do.

"I'll call the garage tomorrow, Marcus," she said. "I didn't think it would start. But thank you so much for helping me today. You're an angel, you know."

Marcus shook his head and lowered his eyes. It was obvious he didn't take praise well. But his eyes were wide and bright when he looked back up at her. "I'll come back and help you anytime," Mrs. Longley," he said.

"Please call me Kath," she told him. "Everybody does. "Now come back to the house with me and I'll give you some money for helping me today."

"No," he said. "You gave me enough yesterday. I like to help you. I'll come back tomorrow."

Kath didn't know what to say, but she thought of Marcus words as she lay there starting to drift into sleep. She was too tired to be anxious and her nightly pill was starting to kick in. Where in the world had this boy come from anyway, and why in the world had he chosen to befriend her?

Her dreams that night were troubling. She was being pursued by someone. Was it Kline? She couldn't be sure, but the terrain took her through dark woods and even in the dream she felt the anxiety cocoon her in a layer of dread. But just before she awoke, she found herself trapped in a log structure. There was no door and no window but high above her was a kind of opening through which sunlight was shining. Perhaps she could climb the wall by finding footholds between the logs. And she did, finding the going much easier than it had appeared, and when she climbed down and looked around her, she wasn't in the woods at all, but right there on the sidewalk in front of her house. And it was spring! The trees along the street were in leaf and the warm air was alive with birdsong.

After awakening she lay for a few moments trying to relax her tense muscles, going from her feet to the top of her head, examining and letting go of what stress and anxiety she could. As she did so she tried analyzing the dream. Had the log structure been the anxiety itself and did her escape from it mean she would eventually free herself from its hold? She could only hope so, and she finally forced herself up with that bit of assurance that all would be well. The first sound she heard from outside was a chainsaw. Someone from the borough had obviously come to remove the tree that had fallen since it had partly covered the street.

She took longer than usual preparing for the day. She had to make some calls and the thought of doing so caused her anxiety to rise and there were traces of panic as she anticipated her actions. This no doubt contributed to her moving so slowly, checking and rechecking every little detail of her shower and the clothes she would wear. Kath particularly dreaded the OCD or obsessive-compulsive disorder that accompanied her condition. Most day she could deal with it well and others when she was particularly high strung and upset, it nearly took possession of her thinking. This morning the condition reached a higher level than usual, and she found that all the containers on the bathroom shelves and sink had to be positioned in a particular way or the anxiety would soar. Finally, with the help of her morning pill she was able to calm enough so that she could make it downstairs.

She fixed a large mug of coffee and sat down at the kitchen table where she had placed her lists from the day before. Before she lifted the phone, she pushed back the curtains and let the sunlight dazzle her eyes with its brilliance. The snow was melting fast. She could hear it dripping down from the roof and it was obvious that the temperature had risen. She felt tears rise in her eyes just then and her hands shook a little. She thought of Fred and how they had often sat together and rejoiced with jokes and laughter when the back of winter broke and they started to look forward to the joys of spring. Were these happy or sad tears, she couldn't be sure, or were they just a part of the anxiety state she suffered? In any case she had to ignore them and get on with the business at hand.

It was past eight o'clock and the market would be open. She tried steadying her hand and picked up the phone and dialed the number. The young lady who answered, Millie Sams, was usually the person who took her orders. She was always quite pleasant, and this morning she actually knew by the sound of Kath's voice who she was. The young girl's tone was pleasant, and she seemed unusually patient while Kath went down her list. It was a particularly long list since she had allowed her stocks to diminish, and before hanging up she added some donuts and cookies and some ice cream in case Marcus would show up again as he had promised. The girl assured her the order would be delivered that afternoon.

Putting down the phone she had to sit for a moment and question why in the world she had thought of Marcus when giving the girl her list. He had refused any food the day before and had only drank some coffee with her. But he was the first person she had actually communicated with in a long time and she had felt comfortable with him. One by one it seemed to her, all her friends had disappeared. Her best friend, Julie Brighton, had moved with her husband to California a few years before. It had been sad that Julie had not been there for her when Fred died, and they communicated now by letter and email, and even that had become a rare thing since her friend was so busy with a career and two children. She had been quite friendly with a few of her fellow professors at the college, but since leaving, none of them had gone out of their way to keep in touch. Communication goes both ways, someone had once told her. You sometimes have to pick up the phone yourself if you want to keep a friendship going.

Now that her call to the market was completed, she phoned Joe's garage without any extra anxiety being added to the mix. Joe himself answered the phone and she could tell by the sound of his voice that he was having a busy morning, and this put her a little on edge. But when she told him who she was his tone changed dramatically. "Oh Mrs. Longley, its good to hear from you. I'm so sorry Fred's no longer with you. He was a good guy. I miss not seeing him. What can I do for you?"

She explained about the car being locked in the garage for months and not starting now and could he possibly have someone come check it. "Sounds like the battery, Mrs. Longley. I'll send Doug over this afternoon with a new one. Once the car's in running order you can bring it in at your convenience and we can check it out and change the oil and everything. After being in the garage for so long it may need a little care."

She thanked him sincerely and after she'd hung up, she sat thinking how lucky she was to still have the market and the garage willing to take personal care of her. Things were changing all around her and she had heard so many horror stories of how life was in the cities and in other towns. Was there any wonder why so many folks took to drugs in order to cope, and why she had turned to alcohol, which she still craved, an even now longed for a glass of wine.

She got up from the table then, her heart racing, and fixed a fresh mug of coffee. The doctor's office was next, and dialing that number was enough to send her into a full-blown attack of panic. But she sat back down at the table breathing deeply. "One step at a time," Fred would tell her when she was worked up and out of sorts. "That's the way you get things done."

She dialed the number and when the phone was answered she didn't recognize the voice of the girl who picked it up. She supposed it was good that the girl didn't seem to recognize her either.

"Is this an emergency, Mrs. Longley? If so, I could get you in this afternoon."

"No, it doesn't have to be today, in fact my car won't start, and I have someone from the garage coming this afternoon. Early next week would work for me. I haven't been in for a few months."

"Yes, I see you missed your last appointment."

"I'm sorry about that. But I will keep this one."

When the call was finished, she sat for a few moments, hands wrapped around the warm cup of coffee, collecting her thoughts. She was happy the doctor's appointment had been made, without any questions having to be answered, without and harshness or finger pointing. Her eyes were eventually drawn to the window where the bright sun that had lifted her earlier seemed to be dimming a bit. She was able to reach and pull back the curtain enough to see the dark clouds that were rolling in from the south. She could tell by the shift in the atmosphere that a change in the weather was imminent. Since the temperature had risen and the snow was melting fast, it seemed they were in for a rainy spell.

And it did rain, for two days straight. Inside the warm cocoon of the house, where she tried to keep busy, organizing the mess of the place and her own mind, Kath was constantly drawn to the windows.

The snow was disappearing as if by magic. Even as she watched it was being washed away by the heavy rain. At the front she saw a constant stream of water rushing toward the culverts that led by the big bridge to Anderson's creek. And the creek was rising, fast it seemed to her. Perhaps it would even reach the street this time, but she was not worried. Things had often been worse in the past and they had had very little to worry about.

Behind the house the hills rose slightly. Streaks of dark land were visible through the quickly melting snow. She could see bits of the macadam trails that led through the township park that adjoined her property. It was quite a large space, beautifully kept, and offered peace and solitude. But because it was only one of three parks in Bridgetown, it seemed to attract far less people. It had only one baseball field which was used by the local high school team, while the other two parks had tennis and volleyball courts, horse shoe pits, and food huts which seemed to attract the younger folks. But Kath was just as happy that their park was more of a quiet place for walking or bird watching. It adjoined woodland on two sides, so there was always some sort of wild life to be seen, even deer who always seemed to cross the township road at the northern end in the madness of deer season to find solace in the wide stretch of woods which adjoined the railroad and was off limits to hunting. She and Fred had walked there often during the early years. One of the trails circled the park in its entirety, leading uphill and down, through woods and grassy spaces, leaving one tired and breathless when it was completed. Other shorter trails had also been laid out, offering exercise with far less effort, but the longer trail began right by their back yard. She had not walked there for nearly two years, but perhaps if she got well, she would attempt it again.

The rain continued through the weekend. On Monday it let up a bit. Her doctor's appointment was for Tuesday afternoon at 2, and by that morning the sun was starting to shine through the few lingering clouds. The man from the garage had come and gotten her car running smoothly again just as Joe had promised. And most of the snow was gone. Just a few dirty traces of it still remained on the hills behind the house and along the hillside on the other side of Anderson's creek under the pine trees which appeared to be a bit droopy after the rain.

Kath had tried not to think about the doctor's visit, but on Tuesday morning she had to do a bit of mental planning. And when she began to anticipate the getting into the car again and driving through a busy part of town to get to the medical building a couple of miles away, she began to feel panic begin to stir. By noon she was in the throes of a major anxiety attack. She was in tears and a cloud of depression fell over her. Dark and ominous, it surrounded her with fear, and she could almost see the doctor shouting and brow-beating her because she had not followed any of his instructions.

She collapsed on the bed and lay there knowing she could not do the doctor's visit. It was too much. She couldn't let anyone see her falling apart. And then a strange thing happened. It seemed to her that she heard the sound of a door opening. Or at least she thought she had. And then she heard Fred's voice, imagination or not, he said quite clearly, "Come on now, let's get up. Just take another pill. I'll go with you."

And somehow the thought of Fred's being there got her on her feet again. Maybe it wasn't real, but it seemed real to her. And they had always gone with each other when they could, to the doctor or dentist or the hospital for tests, and it had always been easier that way and comforting whatever the outcome would be.

She pulled herself together, dressed properly in slacks and a light blue sweater, and went to the kitchen and swallowed a pill. Just before going outside she found a pair of large sunglasses to shield her eyes from the fact that she's been crying and from the sun which was quite bright by this time.

It seemed to her as she finally got into the car and started it up that doing the real thing was far less stressful than all the anticipation she had been experiencing. She was nervous and a bit shaky but had no problem with driving and maneuvering the car onto the street. In fact, all her old skills came back to her almost instantly. Before she knew it, she had arrived at the Medical Center and was safely parked in the parking area.

She imagined Fred opening the door for her, leading her up the walk, opening the door and helping her into the lobby. It was actually an older man who was about to enter, who opened the door, smiled at her and let her go in first. Making her way down the hallway, she arrived at the door to Dr. Barker's suite, breathed deeply, swallowed hard, and went inside.

There were only two people in the waiting area when she entered. A man sat with his eyes closed and a woman was reading a book. The receptionist took her name and gave her a sheaf of papers to fill out. Kath's spirits sank. She hated filling out papers while she waited for a doctor to see her. Her hands always shook, and she found it hard to find answers to the questions the papers asked of her. Noticing her obvious reaction, the receptionist, an efficient looking woman of about forty, smiled at her. "Don't worry, just fill in what you can. If you don't finish just take the papers in with you."

She sat with a clipboard and attempted to answer the questions. How many times before either here or in other places had she answered such things as her parent's health and cause of death? Surely somewhere in their system they should have the answers to such things. Surely, she had gone over these same questions before. She ignored most of it and just answered the basic enquiries as to her identity and current issues. And as she tried to complete the task her anxiety rose to a point where her hands began to shake, and her breathing became ragged. By the time the nurse came from a door at the back to summon her, she was in the throes of a panic attack. She couldn't stop the tears or control the way her body was reacting. Luckily for her, the woman, Mrs. Grant, middle aged and friendly, had been with Doctor Barker for several years, and she knew Fred also and the circumstances of his death.

"Now, Mrs. Longley," she said in a calm voice. "Just try to relax, you're going to be okay. What's going on here? Are you in pain or is it just coming here today that is causing this distress?"

"It's everything," she finally said, attempting to get control of her emotions. "I don't know how I made it here today. I don't know how I'll get home again."

"Of course, you'll get home again. We'll make sure of that," Mrs. Grant said, as she took a blood pressure cuff and gently placed it around her arm. When the reading was completed, she removed the cuff and gave Kath a slightly worried look. "Your pressure is very high today, 170 over 90. I'm sure Dr. Grant will want to retake it when he comes in. Now tell me what's been going on here to get you so upset."

After a moment of Kath's sobbing into her hand, Mrs. Grant handed her a tissue. Once she's calmed a bit, Kath tried in a few sentences to tell her everything, how she had turned to alcohol to get her through Fred's death and how her life had spiraled down into a world of fear and panic so that even leaving the house was a nearly impossible task. And at the end she told her that she was afraid Dr. Barker would yell at her because she had not followed his directions as far as the medication and coming back earlier for regular visits.

"Dr. Barker will certainly not yell at you," Mrs. Grant said, putting her hand on Kath's shoulder. "I know how hard life has been since your husband's death. It was sudden, a shock. It's no wonder you're in the state you are in. But Mrs. Longley, you are not alone. I can't tell you the number of patients we see who suffer the same anxiety you feel right now. Luckily, we know more about it today, it's causes and effects. Dr. Barker is very understanding. You have nothing to be worried about. He'll get to the bottom of this."

Kath thanked her through tears and by the time Dr. Barker entered the room she had calmed enough to at least sit there with some semblance of normalcy. The doctor, a gray-haired gentleman somewhere in his sixties, seemed to have visibly aged since she saw him last. Obviously, his job held more stress that anyone knew. But today he couldn't have been kinder or more sympathetic. He sat in a chair opposite and took her hand. "Now what's this nonsense of being afraid I would yell at you? You must know me well enough to know I would never do that. It might seem like I scold you a bit from time to time, but I am here to help you not to cause you pain or distress. Now tell me how you are feeling right now, today. Let's forget about the past and start over."

Kath struggled at first with her words, but found it easier as she went along, and told the doctor everything, her fear of leaving the house, her problem with alcohol. By the time she was finished she didn't think she had left anything out. Dr. Barker was a good listener. He took a few notes, and nodded his head from time to time, and when she was finished, he sat looking at her, understanding on his face.

"Kath," he said finally, "You've been through a major life change. You've attempted to get through it alone. Obviously, you've turned away from those who could have given you a helping hand. But now I think you realize you need help. And I can give you that with medication and advice. I'm going to prescribe a new medication because you are depressed now, and this sometimes goes hand in hand with the anxiety. And I want you to take this exactly as prescribed. We can reduce the dosage as we go along, but it is very important that you take it properly. No alcohol allowed! I want to check your blood pressure again to be sure you don't need something to help you there."

He placed the cuff on her arm and smiled slightly when he was finished. "It has come down quite a bit," he said. "But I still think you need a mild medication for the hypertension. We'll monitor it. I want you to get a cuff of your own and record the results at home. Bring that list to me when I see you in two weeks. But there is something else Kath, and I am going to insist on this. You need some counseling. I'm going to send you to Jennifer Winston. I should have done it earlier. She's a psychological counselor and she's located right here in the center. She's helped a lot of people and I know she can give you a hand as you work through this. Anxiety is a strange disease at times. But it can be healed."

"Thanks Dr. Barker," Kath said as she got up to leave. "You've been very kind."

Dr. Barker took her hand warmly. "And you've always been a kind person, Kath. Perhaps too kind at times. Sometimes you have to stand up for yourself and let some of the anger you seem to be feeling out! I'll send your new prescriptions to the Bridgetown Pharmacy. They deliver so that you can go right home. They'll call to set up a delivery time."

The relief she felt as she left the center had her breathing deeply. The late February day was washed with sun and the temperature was rising. She had worn only a light jacket and there was an urge to remove it. As she drove away from the center, she thought about what the Dr. had said to her about standing up for herself. Fred had often told her the same thing. And she had tried always to be a nice person. But she had trouble with conflict and tried avoiding it at all costs. She tried never to be angry, but she was coming to realize that sometimes it was still inside her causing harm and needed to be safely released.

She only wanted to get back to a normal life where she could exist without the nagging fear and anxiety that plagued her. Driving along the familiar street toward home she glanced at storefronts she had once entered without fear or trepidation and found herself longing to be able to go into them again. She had a stronger desire than ever before to get well again and she would do everything she could to follow Dr. Barker's orders.

CHAPTER 5

A few days passed and suddenly it was March again. The weather continued to be pleasant with slightly warmer temperatures but with an incessant wind that continued to whip at the trees outside her windows. Before long, it would be spring, and an old desire arose in her to be outside with her hands in the soil once again. Kath had spent the time moving about the house more peacefully, doing everything she could to make the place more shipshape. She was taking her medications just as the doctor had instructed and, only occasionally did she have a desire to go down to the cellar and retrieve one of the remaining bottles of wine Fred had placed there long ago. But she always dealt with the urge by remembering that awful night during the storm when she had awakened in the dark in a state of fear. She didn't want to go there again.

One morning she awoke thinking about Marcus. His face and the sound of his voice came to her gently as she lay there. And then she realized she had been thinking about getting outside again. Sunlight streamed in the window and outside the temperatures had remained warmer than usual. There was work to be done and if the boy came around again she would ask if he might like to be her yard man and help with the mowing and so on. And there was that mess behind the garage to be cleaned up. And then, almost as though she willed it, as she was downstairs in the kitchen fixing herself some breakfast, the door-bell rang. And when she went to the door and opened it Marcus stood there looking at her sheepishly. Kath was shocked to see he had a long scratch all the way down his right cheek and a bruise under his eye. He was dressed in jeans and a jean jacket over a worn looking green tee shirt.

"Marcus, good morning," Kath said. "Come in."

She ushered him inside and down the hall to the kitchen, and when he was sitting at the table, she fixed him a mug of coffee.

"What in the world happened to your face," Kath asked, taking him the coffee and sitting down opposite him at the table.

He was quiet for a moment looking down at the fire engine mug, the fingers of his left hand making a circle on the tabletop.

"Oh, I got into a fight."

"A fight? Who in the world with?"

"Just those boys..."

"Who are those boys?" Kath questioned, realizing she shouldn't cross a certain line with him, but close up the injury to his cheek and eye looked quite nasty. "And what was the fight about? You have quite a bruise you know."

"Oh, they live uptown, and they have a camp over in the woods by the park," Marcus said taking a sip of his coffee. "They caught me over there, one day and beat me up."

"Did you know them, I mean..."

"Yeah I know them. I went to school with them

before. They beat up on me there. There's five of them, and they have like a gang..."

"What is this camp?"

"Oh, they built a kind of shack back there and they get together..."

"What in the world do they do over there, secret meetings? What?"

"I think they do things... Bad things..."

Kath sat for a moment staring at the boy. The look on his face seemed to tell her there were more he wanted to say. It was a look of fear and it was as though he was hiding something.

"Why in the world did you go over there? Sounds like it was dangerous."

"I just wanted to..."

"Did you want to belong?"

Marcus sat quietly, thinking.

"I guess I did at one time but not now," he finally said.

"Did you tell anyone about what they did to you?" Kath asked, nervously stirring her coffee. She knew she should let the subject go, but she could tell by the boy's behavior that he was deeply troubled about something. He was shaking his head and avoiding her gaze.

Marcus finally lifted his eyes and looked at the ceiling and then directly at her. "I should have told someone, I know," he said, fear in his voice. "But they threatened to kill me. I was afraid they would come after me..."

With that Marcus seemed to pull himself together and quickly stood up.

"I came over to see if you wanted me to help you

with something," he said. "It's a nice day out there and I could start working in your yard…"

"Yes," Kath agreed, standing up nervously. "I'll give you a key to the side door of the garage. All the tools are there along the back. You can start by picking up and raking. The wind has blown a lot of debris around this winter. Would you like a job as my yard person this year?"

"Yes, yes I would," Marcus said eagerly. He was about to leave by the back door when he stopped and turned toward her. "Thanks Mrs. Longley," he added. "I'll do the best job I can for you."

Kath stood there at the window, squinting for a moment in the sunlight, and watched as Marcus headed toward the garage. Then she quickly turned away. He was certainly an enigma, she realized. Had she done the best thing by trying to befriend him? But he had befriended her first and on that morning after the storm he had appeared to come from nowhere to her aid. It was almost as though her mind had willed it. She wasn't so sure he had been telling the whole truth about the fight with the boys in the woods. Looking back, his story hadn't rung quite true with her. Over the years as a professor she had learned to listen well. The tone of a voice, the look on the face could easily tell her if someone were lying or even stretching the truth. Her students had taught her well. But in this case with Marcus, even though she doubted his honesty, she would accept him as he was. His help was a gift to her and she would try very hard to just read between the lines with him. She didn't need to know his complete story.

She went into the living room then and turned on the television for the first time in days. She sat down in her lounge chair for a few moments and tuned into the weather forecast. The male commentators voice grated at her nerves, but she forced herself to keep watching. She was slowly acclimating herself to life again and any diversion, including TV would help her.

She was sitting there beginning to feel relaxed when a loud pounding came from the kitchen door. At the same time, she heard Marcus' voice desperately calling her name. She rose quickly from the chair and rushed to the kitchen and flung open the door. Marcus stood there, breathing hard, holding something in his arms. It was a grayish white mass. At first it looked like a clump of snow. And then she realized it was an animal. She saw a tail and a snout with a black nose.

"It's a dog," Marcus exclaimed, excitedly. "It's either sick or been hurt. It was lying back of the garage next to that pile of leaves. At first, I thought it was a pile of dirty snow. What can we do, Mrs. Longley? We have to help it!"

Kath's mind spun. Looking closely at the animal she could see it was still breathing and a whimpering sound was evident. There was a desperate look on Marcus' face.

Kath knew where a veterinarian was located. Out on Birch Avenue. She had passed it many times. It would be a major challenge for her to drive there but if she had to, she was sure she could accomplish it. But there was also a mobile van that she had often seen around town that obviously made house calls. Would the doctor who drove it respond well to an emergency? She rushed into the living room and found a phone book on a table in the corner that Fred had used for his personal desk. Back in the kitchen Marcus was sitting down on a chair rocking the animal in his arms. "You'll be okay," he was saying quietly. "You'll be okay!"

Kath fumbled with the bulky book, and quickly found the listing, Craig Riley, Mobile Veterinarian. She quickly dialed the number. After several rings a male voice answered. "Good Morning, this is Dr. Riley, how can I help you."

The words just seemed to spill from her mouth as Kath explained who she was and what had just occurred. Could he possibly do something to help her?

"I'm over on the other side of town right now," Dr. Riley said, calmly. "But I'm finishing up here. I can be there in half an hour. Cover the dog with a blanket to keep it warm. And try not to worry Mrs. Longley. I'll do what I can."

Kath went quickly into the living room and as though instinctively grabbed Fred's afghan from his chair. He would never use it again and she was sure he wouldn't mind if she used it to cover an animal in trouble. Fred had always been an animal lover. They had had a dog during the early years of their marriage, a poodle named Blackie. It was actually Fred's dog, but she had grown to love it too. When it had died at the age of fifteen, Fred had been so deeply saddened that he would never own another dog. There had only been one Blackie.

She was in tears when she hurried back to the kitchen and covered the dog in Marcus' arms with the afghan. As she did so she could see traces of tears on the boy's face as well.

"The doctor said he would be here in half an hour," She told him. Kath pulled a chair next to his and they sat there quietly, Marcus continuing to cradle the animal in his arms.

"I had a dog once," Marcus spoke finally, a catch to his voice. "He was white to. I called him Sloop. But he was hit by a car and he died in my arms."

Kath patted his shoulder, not saying anything. She prayed that this animal he had found and held would not die in his arms before the Doctor got there. It would be like a repeat of a traumatic experience. Finding the dog had obviously effected Marcus deeply.

The moments dragged by as they sat there, with Kath constantly glancing at her watch. Marcus sat, still rocking the dog, with his eyes closed, a kind of cooing sound coming from his mouth. Nearly fifty minutes passed before she finally was brought to her feet by the sound of the doorbell. She rushed to the door and opened it and found a tall gentleman standing there. Dr. Riley was much younger looking than she had pictured him while they spoke on the phone earlier. She guessed him to be about forty, with dark curly hair and a faint smile on his face. He was dressed casually in khaki trousers and a gray jacket.

"It took longer than I thought it would," he said. "There was some kind of emergency near the center of town and traffic was held up. Where's the dog?"

"Thank you so much for coming," Kath said, quite relieved as she led him into the kitchen. "This is Marcus, he was working for me in the yard and found the dog behind the garage."

"I'll take the dog to the van," Dr. Riley said, taking charge. "All my instruments are there. And you, young man, since you've been taking care of it, can carry it there."

Marcus stood up carefully, trying not to disturb the dog in his arms, and followed Dr. Riley into the living room and out the front door. Kath stood at the window and watched until they entered the van which was parked along the sidewalk just in front of the house. When they were inside, she dropped the curtain and went back to the kitchen. She sat down at the table and cradled her head in her hands. She found herself breathing hard and realized her anxiety was rising. But instead of panicking and fleeing as she often did during such an attack, she faced it, let it come and do its worst. The book she was reading had given instructions on how to do this. Oftentimes she had failed and allowed fear to consume her, but somehow this morning she held the fear at bay with the thought that the attack would pass as it always did.

And it did pass, even though she sat there wondering if the dog could be saved, and if it could what would they do with it? Perhaps the doctor could suggest some options. She didn't feel capable of caring for it herself. Her own issues seemed to be all she could manage at the moment.

After what seemed a long time Kath glanced at her watch and saw that it was nearly forty-five minutes since Dr. Riley and Marcus had taken the dog to his van. She was about to get up and go to the front window when the door bell rang at last. So, she rushed to the door instead and opened it quickly. Marcus entered first, carrying the dog, his face taut and serious. The doctor followed, and Kath led them to the living room where she insisted Dr. Riley take a seat on the sofa. Marcus and the dog sat beside him.

"What we have here is a very sick dog," Dr. Riley

said. "But it's also injured. It's a female West Highland Terrier, probably six or seven years old. Looks like she was beaten or hit by a vehicle. She was either abandoned or escaped from a house somewhere. But's there's no license, identity tag or collar."

"Will she survive, do you suppose," Kath asked, staring at Marcus who was still cradling and petting the bundle in his arms.

"I can't give you a definitive answer at this point," Dr. Riley answered. Right now, she's unconscious. She's obviously dehydrated, has a flea problem and there is a possibility that her hip is broken. If it were up to me, I would probably put her down."

Kath who had sat down in the chair opposite, sighed deeply. She suddenly felt an overwhelming wave of sympathy, not just for the dog but for Marcus who was suddenly shaking his head.

"I could take her with me," Mrs. Longley, the doctor went on. "I would do what I felt was right for the animal. Or you could keep her here overnight and we can see how she is doing in the morning. I've given her antibiotics and some other meds. But that's about all I can do. Since we don't know who the owner is, it's your call."

"I don't know..." Kath blurted, feeling the weight of the moment settling on her shoulders.

"'Don't send her away, Mrs. Longley," Marcus suddenly pleaded. "I'll stay with her and take care of her. We can't let her die!" He sat holding the dog so close to him Kath imagined he would fight the doctor if he tried to take it away.

Well, okay," Kath finally said, her voice wavering. "But how..."

"Get a cardboard box," Dr. Riley said, standing up. "Or just put some blankets here on the floor. Keep her covered and warm. That's all you can do. I'll come back tomorrow and look in on you and see how things are going."

Before making his way to the door, he turned and looked at Marcus and the dog. "Obviously this young man here has a lot to do with whether this animal survives or not," he said, turning to Kath. "His obvious caring and loving attention can make a big difference."

Kath stood at the door and watched until Dr. Riley's van pulled away. For a moment she stood frozen to the spot. It was one of those odd moments she had often had in the past where she didn't want to move because when she did, she knew she would have to go forward and take charge.

Back in the living room finally, Kath sat down again in her chair and stared across at Marcus who was staring back at her, his eyes wide.

"How are we going to do this, Marcus," she finally asked. "It's going to be hard on me here alone, worrying about a sick dog. I'm not sure I can do it."

"I'll stay here with you until she's well again. No matter how long it takes."

It was obvious to Kath that Marcus was not thinking about anything but the welfare of the dog. He had obviously abandoned his normal self and switched into a hero mode where he was sacrificing everything for another. In this case a sick dog.

"But Marcus," Kath went on, "You know you will have to go home. Your parents would be frantic if you didn't show up."

"I could call... them. They won't care."

"I'm sure they will. You'll have to go home before dark." Kath glanced at her watch and saw that it was well past noon. "You can stay with the dog until four o'clock," she said at last. "Then you have to go home."

Marcus was silent for a moment, then he spoke excitedly. "I'll go home and talk to them. I'll explain to them about the dog. I'm sure they'll say its okay if I come back and stay with her tonight."

Kath shook her head. The last thing in the world she wanted to do here was to get into trouble with Marcus's parents. But how could she say no to a boy who obviously cared about nothing more than the welfare of this dog?

Kath said no more but got up and rushed upstairs to a hall closet and found some blankets and another afghan. Back in the living room she and Marcus placed them next to the sofa, making a kind of nest. When it was arranged to Marcus's satisfaction, he placed the dog in it and covered her with one of the blankets. Finally, the boy settled down next to the dog and continued speaking to her in a soft soothing voice.

She went into the kitchen then and sat down again at the table. For a few moments she remained perfectly still and explored her feelings both mentally and physically. She was taut, she was tense, and her mind was riddled with anxious thoughts. Yet somehow the morning medication had held, and the anxiety stayed somewhere outside herself like an invisible ghost ready to appear when least expected.

She was tired, she was hungry, and she suddenly needed a drink. It was all she could do to keep from going to the refrigerator and grabbing the bottle of wine that she knew was there. She did get up finally and went there and opened the door. The bottle lay on a lower shelf so close to her hand. It would be so easy to take it out and open it, but with all her strength she avoided doing so. Instead she took out ham and cheese, lettuce and tomato, a coke and a diet ginger ale, and closed the refrigerator door firmly. Drinking a glass of wine would happen at least for now, only in her imagination.

Kath had no idea when and if Marcus had eaten anything that day. She herself had eaten something, it seemed to her, but what with all that had happened since she couldn't remember what it was. So, she fixed sandwiches and took one on a tray with some cookies, a coke and a container of microwave chicken noodle soup into the living room. Marcus appeared to be asleep, his arm placed protectively around the dog. Kath sat the tray down beside him and gently shook his arm."

"I've brought you something to eat," she said quietly. "You've got to have some lunch."

Marcus didn't move or act like he'd heard her, so she went to the kitchen and ate part of her own sandwich. It seemed dry and tasteless, but she ate dutifully. What in the world was going to happen with Marcus and the dog, she wondered as she sat there nibbling some potato chips? Would it survive and what in the world would happen to it if it did? Marcus said he had had a dog once. Perhaps he could adopt it. But what if someone had lost it and was searching for it? Too many questions, too few answers.

The afternoon passed and at four o'clock Kath went quietly into the living room. Marcus and the dog were obviously still asleep but glancing down at the tray she saw that the sandwich and the cookies had been eaten. The soup hadn't been touched. She gently shook Marcus awake. His head jerked, and he looked up at her with a start, a frightened look on his face.

"You've got to go home now and talk to your parents," she told him. "And if it's okay for you to come back you must bring a note from one of them saying it's okay."

Marcus lay still as death as though he had gone back to sleep and she shook him again, a bit more forcefully. He finally stood up with a sigh. "Do I really have to go," he asked, staring down at the dog. "She needs me."

Kath shook her head. "I'm sure she does, but I have to have your parent's permission first. And I really hope they agree to it because I don't like being here alone tonight with a sick animal."

Marcus made sure the dog was covered well and patted it gently. Standing over them Kath could see the dog was still breathing. And then, quite reluctantly, Marcus put on his jacket and headed for the front door.

"I'll be back," he said. "Make sure nothing happens to her until then."

Kath was silent as she let him out the door. When he was gone a strange silence seemed to envelope the house. After the activity of the past hours she seemed strangely alone. What in the world did Marcus think she could possibly do to keep anything from happening to the dog? She was not prepared to be the animals care giver or Marcus's either for that matter. The boy had come to her as a helper and now it seemed to her, he was becoming something more. For a moment she stood there with her hand on the door knob. It was one of those strange moments again. She closed her eyes tightly as though she could stop time. When she opened them life would start again, and she would have to face it and take charge. Would she have enough strength for the challenge?

CHAPTER 6

It was after dark when Marcus came back. Kath glanced at her watch when the doorbell rang and saw that it was seven o'clock. She went and quickly opened the door and Marcus rushed inside without speaking. He handed her a folder sheet of tablet paper, took off his jacket and went straight to the dog. Kath stood watching as he lifted the blanket and started to rub and speak to the animal. After a moment she opened the paper and read the printed words written in pencil. "I give my permission for Marcus to spend the night and attend to the sick dog." It was signed Peggy Warner.

Marcus lay down next to the dog then and wrapped his arm around it protectively. Kath enquired if he wanted something to eat. When he shook his head, Kath took her own afghan from her chair and lay it over him. Then she quietly went upstairs. It had been an exhausting day, but it wasn't until after she had showered and sat down on the edge of the bed that she realized just how tired she was. Before she knew it, she was lying there on top of the covers her mind drifting between sleep and waking. There was a bit of fear that she was not alone in the house. She should have locked her door, but she didn't have the strength to get up and do it now.

What did she know about the boy really? He had

come to her after a plaintive prayer in the night in which she had asked the universe to help her. But as to his character she knew very little. It was like a series of dots written in pencil that she was trying to connect. But her final thoughts before going totally into a sleep state were wrapped around the fact that Marcus had shown an unusual caring for an injured dog he had found behind her garage. Surely that was enough to win her trust. In her dreams she seemed to be following the boy through a dense dark wood. He appeared to be searching for something, darting here and there, moving the foliage, with his arms, a look of fear and desperation in his eyes.

She awoke to a gray morning. Her first instinct was to get up at once, but she lay there and pulled the covers over her eyes trying to stop time again as she did so. It was after nine o'clock when she finally dressed and went downstairs. A quick glance into the living room showed her that nothing had changed there. Marcus and the dog were just as she had left them the night before. Going quietly into the kitchen she was drawn to the window. Outside, the world was enveloped by rain. The park in the distance was muted by the rain and at places was wrapped in mists and fog. As she stood for a moment watching the rain come down, her spirits fell a bit. She longed for spring, but it seemed one obstacle after another kept her from arriving at her destination.

Feeling a bit anxious she took her morning pills and set about fixing some bacon and scrambled eggs. She made toast and poured some orange juice and then went into the living room to waken Marcus. She was shocked to see he was awake and sitting up. Beside him the dog was awake and had lifted its head. Marcus was speaking to it and encouraging it to stand up.

"Look Mrs. Longley," he exclaimed excitedly noticing that Kath had come to stand beside him. "She woke up. I think she's going to be okay."

Kath was overjoyed to see the small amount of progress that had been made. The dog's eyes were open, and its tail had wagged a bit. "We should give it some water," she said. "And maybe you should take her outside to see if she may have to go to the bathroom."

Marcus stood up and picked the dog up in his arms. Going into the kitchen he hesitated at the door seeing that it was raining, but Kath grabbed an umbrella from the closet and followed him outside. The air was chilly, and the rain was icy on her skin, but she opened the umbrella and held it over the boy and the dog at the edge of the grass. Marcus sat the dog down and it was a bit unsteady on its feet, but it seemed to her that it squatted and after a moment he reached down and gently picked it up again.

Back inside Kath insisted he eat something. Marcus sat down at the table still holding the dog and wolfed down some of the food she had put on his plate. He took a piece of bacon and held it up to the dog's mouth. She sniffed at the bit of meat but didn't eat it.

"What can we feed her, Mrs. Longley," Marcus asked. "Can we get her some dog food?"

Kath's spirits sank. She knew she would eventually have to pull herself together and drive to the pet store out on Avalon Avenue. She could call the market and have them deliver some sort of food for her, but in the meantime, there was some canned chicken in the pantry. Perhaps that would interest her.

When she and Marcus were through with their own breakfast Kath retrieved a can of the chicken, opened it and gave it to the boy. Marcus took a bit of it in his fingers and held it up to the dog's mouth. At first it turned its nose away, but he was persistent and eventually it opened its mouth and took in a small bit of the food. One small bit of chicken, but it was a hopeful sign and Marcus threw her a look of triumph.

"What will we do with her," Marcus finally said, rubbing his hand slowly across her back. "She's been badly treated wherever she came from. She has cuts and lumps under her fur."

"I don't know, Marcus," she answered. "We'll have to talk to Dr. Riley when he gets here later. What if she got out of a house somewhere and her family is searching for her?"

"The doctor told me yesterday in the van that he thought she's been beaten and that she may have been out in the cold for a long time," Marcus replied. "He said she was underweight and that she needed to be spayed. He said she could have been used for breeding."

For a moment Kath sat wondering if Marcus had really heard the doctor correctly. It brought back the worry that he might be capable of stretching the truth a bit. But a couple of hours later when Dr. Riley showed up to check on the dog, she brought up the subject.

The doctor and Marcus were about to take the dog to the van. Outside, the rain was still coming down and they had covered the animal with a blanket.

"Could the dog really have been used for breeding," She asked, standing in the doorway.

"All the signs are there," Mrs. Longley. "She hasn't

been spayed and obviously she's had puppies in the past."

Kath sat in the living room brooding over the animal's future, waiting for the two of them to return. If they couldn't find the place or people for whom the dog belonged, perhaps Marcus could take her. It was obvious he had a deep love for animals. She couldn't possibly keep the dog. It was all she could do at this point to keep herself on her feet, let alone take care of a lost animal.

"She's a very lucky dog," Doctor Riley told her when he and Marcus returned from the van. "She's awake and her temperature has come down. I think her hip is just badly bruised and not broken. If Marcus hadn't found her yesterday, I'm afraid she would be dead by now. I really think she's been beaten and very badly treated. In a few days she should be out of danger."

"A few days?" Kath shook her head. "I couldn't possibly keep her. What about you Marcus, could you take her home with you?"

"Oh no," Marcus spoke quite sharply. "My parents would never agree to my having a dog."

"But before Marcus found her, she obviously belonged to someone. Couldn't we check around? Maybe someone will put out a message about a missing dog."

"That's possible," the doctor told her. "And in my rounds, I'll check the shelters and so on. If I find out anything, I'll get back to you. In the mean time you would be doing the most human thing to keep her here for the time being. You obviously have this young man to help you. I'm afraid it might me a bad thing if we moved her now. Your kindness and your warm house have obviously helped her along the path to healing."

"But what about food? That kind of thing?" Kath's voice seemed to rise a few decibels and suddenly seemed shaky.

"Don't worry about that. I'll leave you a list of products you can use. I have a recipe for a chicken and rice dish I've often used for sick dogs. I would suggest a medium sized cage. You can buy one down at the pet store. They're quite inexpensive. She would be very comfortable in that with some warm blankets. And I'll get back to you in a day or two."

The doctor left her the list he had mentioned along with some medications the dog should be given. Then he said goodbye without giving her a chance to protest. After he'd gone, Marcus sat down on the sofa with the dog and Kath sank into her chair and stared for a moment at the floor. Whether or not she liked it she would have to gather the strength to go out and do some shopping for the dog. She closed her eyes for a few seconds and scanned her mental and physical strength to see if she was up to the task. The medications her own doctor had given her had helped to build a line of defense around her as far as the anxiety was concerned. Buying a cage for the animal seemed like a good idea. After all Marcus could not be there all day long, and it would help her feel more at ease. She finally made up her mind that she would attempt the mission as soon as she could get herself together. She would have to trust Marcus to stay with the animal until she returned. She finally sat up and told the boy what she planned to do.

Hearing her words, Marcus's face broke out in a smile. "And do you think you could get her a collar and lease," he asked. "That way she can be safe when we take her outside."

By the time Kath had donned her coat, grabbed and umbrella and sloshed through the rain to the garage, she was shaking. She sat in the car for a few moments, her hands held firmly on the steering wheel, allowing a sense of unsteadiness and fear to pass. She had a sudden urge to run back to the safety of the house. But she remained determined and once the car had warmed a bit she drove out of the garage and into the street.

She made it safely to the shopping plaza and entered the pet store with only a slight feeling of light-headedness. She took a cart and within a short period of time was able to find everything she needed. She chose a pink collar which she hoped would fit, and a matching leash. A male clerk passed her in the aisle and she stopped him and asked where the cages could be located. Not only did he help her find one, conveniently packaged in a large flat box, but once she had checked out, he helped her with it through the rain to the car and placed it in the back seat.

There was a strange sense as she drove back toward home, that nothing was real. She seemed out of herself somehow, almost as though she were above the car, somewhere in the rain, looking down. But it was not as though she were falling apart, it was as though she were trying to come back to herself and enter the bubble of peace she had finally located at the center of herself.

Marcus was quite exited when she returned. The dog was lying on its side, covered with the afghan, her head exposed.

"She ate some more chicken, Mrs. Longley. And she drank some water. I think she's going to be alright!"

The dog raised its head and looked toward her. Kath

noticed how clear her eyes were since the day before. There was an odd look of intelligence there, but also a sense of wariness and fear. Marcus petted her head and she looked up at him as though she knew he was attempting to help her.

Kath sent him to the car then to retrieve the things she had purchased earlier. By this time the rain had slowed to only a slight drizzle, so the task was easily accomplished. Both she and the dog watched as Marcus took the parts of the cage from the box and assembled it, placing it finally in a spot next to the sofa. He placed the blankets inside and then spoke to the dog before he sat her in it.

"You'll be okay in here," he soothed. "We won't close the door. Only at night."

The dog, seeming to understand, went into the cage dutifully, and settled down in a far corner. She lay there and stared back at them calmly. It was as though she felt safe in the cage and was pleased with it.

"You should go home now, Marcus." Kath finally told him. "You must talk to your parents and let them know what's going on. We can't have them worrying, can we?"

"Oh, they won't be worried, Mrs. Longley," Marcus told her, his attention totally on the dog. He was sitting protectively in front of the cage, he and the dog staring at each other as though they were communicating telepathically. "She really likes the cage," he told her. "But she wants me to let the cage door open."

Reluctantly Marcus did leave her shortly after that. The dog had fallen asleep and lay curled in a ball at the far end of the cage. It slept away the afternoon and didn't awaken until Marcus returned just before dark.

Sensing that Marcus had come back the dog rose to her feet and slowly came to him. Came out of the cage without his assistance and then stood silently while he attached her collar and leash and led her out to the kitchen door. The dog's gait was a bit slow and there was a limp as she walked, but she went confidently, trustfully. She was still dirty and badly in need of a bath and grooming. But she was still alive, and Kath realized if Marcus had not been there the poor animal would be still lying stiff and dead behind her garage. A sharp pang of anxiety went through her at the very thought and Kath realized how sensitive she still was. Would she ever get to the place where her body would not react to just a slight twist in her thinking?

The routine of Marcus coming in the morning and taking care of the dogs needs continued for several days. He would go away for the afternoon and then return at night. Kath would fix the doctors formula of chicken and rice and the dog would eat it, gobbling it up as though it was constantly starved. Dr. Riley visited every couple of days, seeming very pleased that the dog had come back from near death. He instructed Marcus on how to try giving the dog a bath. Marcus followed his instructions and the dog cooperated unusually well, returning to her cage once he had dried her well, and quickly fell asleep. When Kath questioned Dr. Riley if he had heard anything from anywhere about a missing dog, his answer was always the same.

"I have heard nothing about that, Mrs. Longley," he would say and shake his head. "There is talk about an irreputable man who runs a puppy mill over in the next township. They tell me he doesn't really care for his animals and he's been turned in to the law several times. I am a bit suspicious that she may have stopped producing puppies and he just sat her out to fend for herself."

One day after a brief visit, Dr. Riley smiled at her and shook his head. "Well Mrs. Longley it seems to me that you have inherited a pet. With Marcus's help I think you will do very well with her."

"But what if she does belong to someone..."

"If she did, we would have heard about it by now," the doctor told her. "Give me a call in a few weeks and we'll get her caught up with her shots. Until then it's all in your hands, Mrs. Longley."

Marcus was not there on that particular visit, but when he did return, she told him what the doctor had said. Of course, he was overjoyed. The dog came from the cage to greet him as it always did when he came back, and he fell to his knees and hugged it hard. "You know I'll help you with her," he said. "She needs us Mrs. Longley! But I was thinking, we will have to give her a name. What do you think?"

Kath just shook her head. She was having a hard time wrapping it around her head that this dog was now her responsibility. She was not prepared to decide on a name for her. Marcus would have to do that himself.

It was on an evening in early April just at dusk when a strange thing happened. Kath had been expecting Marcus to return. He had dutifully spent the nights with the dog, sleeping on her sofa, covered with sheets and blankets she left for him. He had taken to just slipping in the kitchen door, and the dog always greeting him with a bark, alerting her even before he came into the house, that he was there.

But this evening the front doorbell rang and Kath who was sitting on the sofa saw that the dog was sitting up, its ears quite alert and she heard a low growl coming from the cage. A sharp pang of anxiety ran along her back as she got up to answer the door. She turned on the porch light and looked through the window and saw a strange man standing there. A chill ran through her when she saw him. It was the stern angry kind of look he gave her when he saw her through the window. He was tall, though a bit thin and wore a green flannel shirt over a pair of jeans. She guessed his age at about fifty and he was a bit hunched over, wringing his hands nervously.

Kath thought for a moment that she shouldn't answer the door, but then decided she had better do so in case the stranger was in some sort of trouble. Along the street the lights had come on and there was a kind of safety in the way they shone out toward the impending dark.

Kath quickly opened the door. She didn't intend to ask the man in. "How can I help you, she asked, trying to keep her voice steady and calm.

"Who are you," the man asked sternly, the pungent smell of alcohol coming from his mouth as he spoke.

Thinking it was a strange question for someone to ask who had just appeared at her door, she spoke robotically. "I'm Kathleen Longley," she answered. "And who are you?"

"I'm Bart Warner, Marcus's father. I've come to find out what he's been doing here. He hasn't been home nights and I followed him one night and saw him slipping in the back there. He's only thirteen, you know. What is a woman of your age doing with him? He's only a boy. Seems a bit strange if you ask me. What's really been going on here?"

The man's tone in questioning angered Kath. She spoke quickly, "Why it's the dog, didn't he tell you that? He found a dog behind my garage while he was doing some yard work for me. He told me he asked if it was okay. Didn't he tell you?"

"He told me nothing." Bart Warner said angrily. "I just think you…"

"But his mother sent me a note stating it was okay. She seemed to understand about the dog."

"His mother?" Bart Warner stood there silently for as moment swaying from side to side. It was though he had been shocked by her words. He let out a strange laugh.

"His mother?" He finally got out. "His mother walked out on us two years ago!"

"But he talked about his mother all the time," Kath said defensively. "I just assumed…"

"Don't assume anything where Marcus is concerned," Bart Warner said angrily. "He's mentally challenged, didn't you know that? He's a thief and a liar. He was thrown out of school for his lying. And he has anger issues. He's always beating up on the other kids…"

Kath was shocked to the bone by what this man was telling her. She felt like she was no longer able to stand up. This was crazy. This man was describing someone she didn't know. How could he be describing Marcus? "I had no idea," was suddenly all she could get out.

"No idea? But you've been taking part in his games. You've been shielding him. I have a good idea of turning you into the law. You've been taking advantage of a juvenile. Why what you're doing is child abuse. I'll take steps…"

"Take whatever steps you need to," Mr. Warner."

Kath said angrily, her hand firmly on the door handle. "I've done nothing to harm your son. Whatever you are thinking is wrong. It's cheap and dirty and you should be ashamed. But I can assure you I will not allow him to spend another night in this house."

Kath stepped inside quickly, slammed the door and closed the curtains. For a moment she stood against the door breathing hard. When she had enough courage to lift the curtain again and look out, Bart Warner was gone. She breathed a bit easier and went into the living room and sat down on her chair. Nearby, in its cage, the dog looked up at her, its eyes wide. Then it looked in the direction of the kitchen as though it was expecting Marcus to come through the door at any moment.

What in the world was she going to do with the dog now that Marcus would have to stay away? She had grown used to his being there. He had been kind to her and the dog. He had done everything she had asked of him and more. Of course, she had expected his stretching of the truth, but the shock of finding out that his mother was no longer in his life and that he had spoken of her as though she was, seemed more than she could comprehend. He's mentally challenged, his father had said. But now all Kath could feel for him was pity.

Kath sat there, eyes closed, anxiety rising around her in a dark wave. Life had been complicated before the arrival of this boy who she had often seen as a gift from the universe. Now how could she think of him as a fraud, as a trickster who had torn apart her house of cards?

She finally managed to get up from the sofa and head for the kitchen. She went directly to the refrigerator and retrieved the bottle of wine from the bottom shelve. Even before she uncorked it, she could only think of the feeling of calm it would leave her with, the bliss of it. But when she did manage to open the bottle, her hands shaking badly, and take a first sip of the liquid she had poured into a paper cup, the taste was shockingly bitter, and the rush of it burned her throat, causing her to spit out what remained in her mouth and pour the remainder of the wine still in the cup, down the sink.

CHAPTER 7

Shocked by her reaction at the taste of the wine, Kath sank into a chair at the table and grabbed a tissue from the box beside her. It seemed that tears ran from her eyes at any moment these days and there were even more of them now that her trusted alcoholic friend had failed her. She sat there breathing deeply, her eyes closed, until the worst of the anxiety had lifted. When she opened them again, she was startled to see that the dog had come to the kitchen from its cage and stood by the door wanting to go out.

This was usually the time that Marcus always took her out for a bathroom break, and the dog was looking up at the door as though expecting him to come in or for it to open. Marcus had conveniently placed the dog's leash on a hook next to the door, and although Kath was feeling nervous and shaky, she stood up and dutifully attached the leash to the dog's collar.

"I'm sorry I'm not Marcus," Kath spoke as soothingly as she could. "But you will have to put up with me now. I'll do my best to take care of you. Sometimes in life we have to adjust to new ways."

She switched on the outside light and followed the dog outside to the yard. It was a slightly chilly evening, the air tinged by the scents and stirrings of spring. Above her the sky was strewn with stars and while she followed the dog's limping gait across the grass, she stared up at the infinite space and said a silent prayer that the whole awkward situation with Marcus would be resolved and peacefully dealt with. Just before going back inside she realized she would have to confront the boy at some point and let him know how badly she felt that he had deliberately lied to her when all she had tried to do was befriend him. Obviously, his father had kept him home tonight, perhaps he had locked him in his room, but she was sure he would come back to her at some time. His affection for the dog would be the magnet that would summon him.

Once inside the house and she had removed the dog's leash, it headed straight to the cage and Kath followed. The dog went to the back corner, circled around and lay down with a sigh. For a moment Kath sat staring at the animal. It sat there almost regally, ears straight in the air as is the natural habit of the Westie dog. But in this case the animal's right ear was bent over at the end, giving it a natural birth mark. As she sat there her attention on the animal, she realized that what Marcus had been right when he told her that she needed a name. The name Marcus, she was sure, was of Roman derivative. Mars was a warrior, the God of war in Astrology. What female name could she think of that would fit the dog? The thought spun in her head for a moment and then she remembered the name of one of her female students. It was Cassandra and when she questioned the young lady as to the name's origin, she had told her that the name was Greek, and Cassandra had been a Trojan prophetess. Cassandra. Marcus and Cassandra. Somehow the combination seemed just right to her so Cassandra would be it.

"Your name is now Cassandra," Kath spoke softly to the dog just before she made her way upstairs at bedtime. "I think it suits you. But you must forgive me that I am having a hard time with your being here. I will come around in the end I am sure. I wish Marcus could have named you. I wish he could be here with you tonight. But maybe he'll come back to see you soon."

She thought of Marcus when she went to bed later. What kind of life he had with his father, what kind of psychological problems did he have that his father had told her he was mentally challenged? And then the last hurdle she could not find a way over was why had he lied to her about his mother, and had even written her a note supposedly from her that said he could stay with the dog? And when she finally fell into a troubled sleep, Marcus's father blocked her path with a pointing finger and a face filled with pure evil.

In the morning, despite her troubled sleep, Kath was able to get out of bed just as the clock on the bedside stand read 7 Am. She went down to the kitchen and fixed herself coffee. She sat at the table for a moment and stared out the window where a weak sun was peeking through layers of mists spread across the park in the distance. She was a bit startled when something nudged her leg and she looked down to see the dog, Cassandra, staring up at her.

"I guess you want to go outside already," Kath said reluctantly, realizing that this was obviously going to be a regular ritual and she would have to get used to it. She got to her feet at once and attached the dog's leash. Outside there was a slight chill to the air and she wished she had worn her sweater, but she followed Cassandra around the perimeter of the yard, in her mind imagining the fence she wanted to build. If it were in place now, she could just open the back door and let the dog roam at will. She would do some research soon and contact a refutable company to come take a look at the property and give her an estimate.

She was about to lead Cassandra back into the house when out of the corner of her eye she saw a figure approach her from the street. It was Marcus, and Cassandra let out a loud bark of greeting. It was the first time she had heard the animal bark as loudly. Marcus, looking a bit ragged in an oversized sweat shirt, his hair uncombed, fell to his knees in front of the dog. The dog was all over him in an instant, licking his face and showing no sign of a bad hip as she stood on hind legs in an obvious state of bliss. Marcus spoke to her in words Kath could not quite hear or understand, but she relinquished the leash and as she was about to go inside, she said, trying to keep her words as calm as possible, "I've named her Cassandra."

"Cassandra, that's a pretty name," he said, stroking the dogs head.

She was sitting at the table a few minutes later, trying to think of what she would say to Marcus and how she would control her anger when a hesitant knock came to the kitchen door. Normally Marcus would have entered without knocking but he must know about his father's visit and what he had told her. She quietly told him to come in. Once he had taken the lease from the dog he sat down opposite at the table.

"You shouldn't be here," Kath said, "Your father doesn't want it."

"I know," Marcus finally told her, his head staring

down at the table where he was wringing his hands. "He told me never to come here again."

"Then why did you come?"

"Because I couldn't stay away from...Cassandra, and...you," he said, his words barely audible. "He says things sometimes that he doesn't mean. He's an alcoholic, you know, but when he's sober..."

"Yes, I know he was drinking last night when he was here. I could smell it on him. And he said terrible things to me, about you, about your staying here at night, he insinuated bad things..."

"What things?"

"He said you have mental issues," Kath said hesitantly. "He told me you lie and have anger problems."

"Those are his issues," Marcus said quickly and angrily. "He's a drunk. He was mean to my mother. He beat up on her and on me. That's the real reason she left. She couldn't stand the way he treated us."

"What does your father do," Kath asked. "I mean what kind of a job does he have?"

"He used to work on the railroad, but he's disabled now. He fell out of an engine. I think he was drunk."

"Is he the one who put those marks on you? The ones on your arms and and on your face when you first came here?"

"Maybe..."

"Did he do it or didn't he," Kath said, going back to the coffee maker to refill her cup. She made an extra mug and sat it in front of Marcus.

"We fight all the time," Marcus spoke again. "I'm so used to it I don't remember who hit who. I get him back!"

"But Marcus that's no way to live. Why don't you tell someone? Try to get some help?"

"Because if I complained and they saw how I live they would send me somewhere. I don't want to go away, to a strange family, a strange place. I used to think about it, but now..."

"But now?"

"I don't want to go away from Cassandra... and you! And if my mother came back and I wasn't there..." Marcus began to cry, his face wet with tears.

There was silence between them for a moment. Marcus took a tissue from the box and began wiping at his face. Kath wanted to reach out across the table to comfort him, but she held back. Some anger still seethed in her and she had her own challenges to face. But she suddenly brought up her own concerns for herself and for Marcus.

"I want to help you, Marcus," she said firmly, "but your father threatened to turn me into the law for shielding you..."

"He won't turn you in to anybody. He's too scared himself for that!" Marcus sat up straight and sudden color rushed to his face. "He knows he can't control me though he tries. I do what I want, and I go where I want to go. If I went to the law, he would be sorry..."

Marcus was silent suddenly as though there was more he wanted to say but didn't. Kath looked into his eyes and saw something that scared her. Was it anger, was it something deeper, a mental problem that even he didn't understand?

"First of all, Marcus," Kath finally spoke, "You can't go on getting into physical fights with your father. What if he really hurt you? What if your bruises and scratches turned into breaks or serious injuries? You've got to stop it. And you've got to stop lying!"

Marcus looked up at her warily. He knew she was about to let him know how she really felt.

"You came to me when I really needed your help," Kath began. "And I've grown fond of you. But I'm still not able to grasp the lies you told me about your mother, that she's still there, that she holds you together. You even wrote a note and signed her name making me believe it was okay for you to spend the night and take care of Cassandra. Do you realize that even the smallest lie has consequences?"

Marcus sat there looking down into his coffee mug and shook his head. He didn't seem to know what to say.

"Do you even understand why you told me that lie," Kath asked, trying to keep her voice steady.

"I guess I lied abut my mother because I wanted her to be there, I wanted her to come back." Marcus spoke with a new tone, one she had never heard from him before. He spoke in a child's voice and it was obvious to her that he was vulnerable and had always been. He had lost the one person who had protected him. Perhaps Kath understood why he had lied about it.

"But you've got to stop lying to me." She said. "I want to be your friend. I'll help you if you let me, but I won't tolerate any more lies. I grew up believing honesty was the best policy. One lie leads to another and in the end you get caught up in trying to find the truth. Do you understand that?"

"I guess I do... It's hard though."

"I know this, but you've got to promise me you will always be honest with me. If you aren't, I'll have to say goodbye to you. Do you promise you'll try?"

Marcus looked from side to side and reached down

to rub Cassandra's head. She had come to sit silently by his side. Finally, he spoke, his voice wavering. "I'm sorry, I'll try."

"You can come here as you like." Kath said finally, relieved. "You'll have to deal with your father and his reactions, but you can visit Cassandra and me whenever you want. I'm not worried about your father and what he thinks. If he comes here again, I'll know how to deal with it. But you can't spend the night with us. He tried to turn that into something bad and dirty. In the meantime, we'll think about what we can do to make your life better."

In the days ahead Marcus's visits were sporadic, but he came every day. As the weather improved, he took over all the yard work and began to help Kath as she was able to spend time out of doors without becoming anxious or feeling overwhelmed by worries. He would take Cassandra into the park itself and the dog would always look forward with joy to his visits. The April weather was splendid, days of warm sun and occasional rain but the trees were in leaf again and the blossoms along the street were spectacular. The violets in the grass, long parades of them, caused her to be misty eyed.

She did make a startling discovery one afternoon when she decided to sit on the front porch for a few moments. Her porch furniture was gone, and the space was empty! It had been a set of brown wicker, a sofa and a chair, along with a round matching table. It had sat on the front porch for as long as she could remember, except for the winter months when Fred had always taken them back to the garage for protection. Kath felt terrible realizing the furniture was gone. She had loved sitting there on quiet afternoons; she and Fred had often sat there together, discussing their days and how they had been spent. The scents and sights of the stream across the street always vied for their attention.

Who could have taken the furniture and what should she do about it? It seemed to her it was something old man Kline next door might do just to be evil. He could have managed it since the furniture was not unusually heavy and he was fit enough to accomplish the theft. She decided to call the police station and report the missing items. The officer she talked to was very sympathetic, but he gave her little hope of their recovery. "We've had a lot of reports this year about stolen furniture and yard ornaments. But I'll make note of the theft. Give us a call if you find anything else missing."

The very next day she found the number of a fence company in the phone book and arranged for a man to come and give her an estimate for the fence she wanted to build around her property. Old man Kline had taken several opportunities to spy on her, especially when Marcus was in the yard with the dog or when he was behind the garage bagging up the leaves Kline had obviously placed there. Kath would notice the curtains move in his back window, or notice him skulking about his own garage, eyes peeled in her direction. On the day that the fence man came, and she went into the yard to show him what she wanted, Kline seemed to be everywhere at once, up and down his driveway, viewing the progress from all angles, no doubt alerted by the logo of the fence company emblazoned on the van he was driving.

Mr. Lewis, the man from Breyer Fence, was very efficient and thorough. He helped her to decide on a 6-and-a-half-foot fence constructed of sections of treated boards along the edge of the driveway, and a six-foot chain-link fence around the house and yard itself, with matching gates placed at front, side and back. Noticing Mr. Kline's pacing as he and Kath talked, he took her on to the porch where he lowered his voice and shook his head. "Look's like you have the kind of neighbor who may not be liking the idea of your building a fence. I would recommend that you have your property surveyed before we go through with this. That way you can avoid trouble in the future. I have a surveyor I work with who would be able to do this for you reasonably."

Kath agreed to having the survey, and there was a certain satisfaction she felt over the idea of the fence. If her neighbor would have shown her some cooperation and respect it wouldn't have had to be done. But now that Cassandra had come to live with her it would make her life easier and would also protect the dog in so many ways. There was a sense of deep satisfaction that held her anxiety at bay when the van finally pulled away that morning.

It was near the beginning of May when the doctor's office called. Marcus had come and was outside with Cassandra, and Kath was fixing them some breakfast when the phone rang.

"This is Dr. Barker's office calling to confirm your appointment tomorrow at two. Are you going to be able to make it?"

Kath's mind was numb for a moment. They had made an appointment for her when she was at the doctor's before. Had it been a month already? The very thought of going again filled her with dread.

"I'm glad you called," Kath finally managed to get out. "Otherwise I probably would have missed it."

"The doctor also wants you to see Jennifer Winston when he's finished with you. She has the afternoon free and he feels it will be a good time."

It took a few moments after the call for Kath to bring the whole thing into focus. She had driven to see Dr. Barker before when she was feeling far worse than she did today. Yet now the anxiety she was feeling seemed just as bad as before. Anticipating an event was always far worse than the real thing, she realized. It was as though the slightest touch of the switch flooded the mind with panic.

The next day turned out to be beautiful weather-wise. The world had been washed by Spring and everywhere she looked as she drove to the medical center there were glimpses of the season, pale green trees, long vistas of flowers in every shade and hue, and folks out of doors tending to chores or just sitting or strolling, enjoying the new-found freedom of the season. If she felt good enough on the way home, she might stop at the garden center and pick up a few geraniums for the pots at the back. Marcus could help her get them going. In other years before Fred died, she might have gone crazy buying flowers and bushes. But this was not one of those good years. They were gone forever, and Fred's absence had left her like a fragile leaf about to fall from the tree.

She was feeling rather low by the time she finally arrived at the doctor's office. When Dr. Barker stepped into the room where she was waiting, he gave her a long serious look as though he could tell how she was feeling. Still he greeted her warmly. "You look as though you're feeling much better than the last time I saw you," He said, glancing down at the notes the nurse had left for him. Your blood pressure has come down nicely. How are you feeling otherwise?"

"I'm coping," was all she managed to say.

"It seems to me the medication must be doing its work," Dr. Barker said then. "At least you seem in better control of your emotions this time. And how have you been doing as far as the drinking?"

"I've stopped that," she said. "I felt I had to. I was getting out of control."

"Well good for you! And you're going to see Mrs. Winston today, aren't you?"

"They told me I have an appointment when I'm finished here."

Yes, you do, and I think this is a good time for you to be seeing her now that you've gotten stronger. She can help you in many ways."

When the doctor was finished with her, she left his office and found her way down a long hall to where a sign on a door announced, Jennifer Winston, Counseling Services.

Stepping inside she saw that the waiting room was empty. A receptionist took her information and told her to sit down, Mrs. Winston would be with her in a moment. Some soft music was playing in the background and Kath began to lose the sense of anxiety and tenseness that always came to her at meeting a new person or situation. By the time Mrs. Winston herself came through the door at the back she was quite a bit more relaxed. Kath was a bit surprised to find that Jennifer Winston was not at all the woman she had imagined. She had expected a middle-aged lady with glasses and gray hair. Instead the woman who greeted her was probably in her mid-thirties, very young looking with dark wavy hair and a glowing complexion. She wore a flowered dress and a light blue sweater. And she was just as friendly as she appeared.

"It's so nice to meet you," Mrs. Longley," she told her when they had entered a comfortable looking room where two chairs sat together in a corner. There were bright paintings on the wall and green plants and fresh flowers had been placed on a table near a window. "And it's nice to meet you as well," Kath said when they were seated on the chairs next to each other. She had expected to be sitting in front of a stern looking woman at a desk.

"I'm so sorry to hear that your husband has passed," Mrs. Winston said sincerely, once she made sure that Kath was comfortable. "How long has he been gone?"

"It's over a year now," Kath told her.

"And what are you feeling right now? Depression, anger? The doctor's notes tell me you are suffering panic and anxiety. Are you feeling any better at all?"

Jennifer Winston's kindness and obvious caring soon had Kath calmer and much more able to let her true feelings come through. She related as much as she could of her difficulties, up to the night of the storm and how she felt as though she wanted to die that night.

"Anxiety and panic are born out of difficult life events," Mrs. Winston told her when Kath had reached a lull in her story. "In your case your retirement and your husband's death. But I have found something else to be true in most cases. The person suffering nervous illness is usually fair minded, good and kind who does her best to get along with others. But in doing so she is too nice, too kind, and can be taken advantage of. I think a little of that is in play here. Anger can easily build up and if not released can cause havoc with the nervous system. Who are you angry with, Mrs. Longley?"

Kath thought for a moment before speaking. "Well right at the moment I'm angry with my neighbor," she said, and then was able to relate some of it, up to her decision to build the fence.

"Anybody else?" Mrs. Winston asked.

"Well yes," Kath said. "There's an old lady, Geraldine Harvey, who lives a few blocks from me who calls me Mrs. Lonely and dislikes me intensely for no reason at all, and the professor at the college who treated me so badly I decided to retire." She paused for a moment, scanning her mind and suddenly a light of recognition flashed, and she found herself suddenly in tears and began to tremble.

"Why are you crying," Mrs. Winston asked sympathetically, offering her a tissue from a box on the table. "What were you thinking just then."

"I realized I am angry at my husband, Fred."

"And why would that be Mrs. Longley?"

"Because he died and left me!" Kath suddenly covered her face with her hands and continued to sob as though saying such a thing was terrible of her.

"My dear, its perfectly okay for you to be angry at your husband," Mrs. Winston said quietly. "Even though he didn't mean to die and he's not here for you to tell him how you feel, somehow we believe it's not proper for us to be angry at the dead."

When Kath removed her hands from her face and was breathing easier, Mrs. Winston went on with what she was saying. "Did it ever occur to you that you should let those people know that they've hurt you by behaving as they have? Not in a confrontational way of letting your anger burst through like a volcano, but by calmly stating the facts to them face to face. It may not even phase them but for you it can work wonders in clearing some of the debris of the anxiety and anger that has built up in you. Of course, you can't speak to your husband face to face, but perhaps you can write him a letter, or when you are alone somewhere and are thinking of him, speak to him calmly, let your voice be heard, and let him know what you are thinking, good or bad. Then believe in your heart that he has heard you."

Kath sat during the rest of the session marveling at Jennifer Winston's calm demeanor. The peaceful look never left her face. No matter what she might say, what thought she tried to describe to her, the counselor kept a kind sympathetic attitude throughout. When she spoke, Kath tried to emulate her calmness of voice, her gentle way of keeping her hands calmly in her lap, not pointing and gesturing as Kath herself seemed to be doing lately.

When the hour of the session was up Kath asked Mrs. Winston how she kept her sense of calm despite having to listen to someone who could get quite emotional as she had done.

"I just try to remember that I am focusing outwardly on a person who is trying to find a way through a difficult place, and I keep my mind off my own thoughts and feelings. And I practice a meditation technique. It really helps to keep me grounded. Before you leave, I'll give you a paper on meditation. It will describe a simple one which will help you get started. In the meantime, just keep doing what you are doing. Exercise, activity, and gradually working yourself out into the world again will go a long way. I'll see you again in a month and we'll see how you are doing."

Mrs. Winston hugged her warmly as she was leaving the room. Getting into the car in the parking lot, Kath felt buoyed by the experience of visiting a counselor for the first time. As she had come to realize so often, during this awful period of anxiety and panic, the thought in a tired mind of doing something was far worse than the experience itself. Driving toward town, the sunlight through the window and the sights and sounds of spring everywhere she turned, had her feeling, at least for a few brief moments, that she was well again.

As Kath approached the garden center, she slowed the car. She suddenly felt strong enough to stop, go inside and purchase a few things, and leave quickly. She pulled into the parking area and was pleased to see that the place was not as busy as she imagined it would be. She grabbed a cart and went inside. A heavy-set lady in a wide straw hat and a pink dress that was far too tight blocked her path as she tried to get into the first aisle, but she breathed deeply and smoothly made her way around the obstacle. She picked up a bag of potting soil, some plant food, and a couple of hand tools which she seemed always to be losing. Then she went through a door at the back, out to a larger greenhouse where most of the plants were in well-organized rows. There were several shoppers there, carts loaded with assorted plants, who didn't seem to worry that as it often did the spring weather might suddenly turn cold and spoil their efforts. She remembered in past years how often there would be frost warnings and she would find herself outside as it was growing dark, covering her own efforts with newspapers and sheets.

Kath chose six geranium plants of medium size, two red, two white and two pink. This would be enough to get her started again. Her garden club days were behind her and what she really longed for, now that spring was unfolding all around her, was time in the sun, sitting on the front porch or on the back patio, reading or doing nothing. It suddenly made her remember her missing porch furniture and she winced. Should she buy some new things? No, she would make do with the five or six folding lawn chairs Fred had stored away in the garage. Marcus could help her get things organized. Another year perhaps, she might think of buying something new.

Kath was feeling confidant yet still a bit nervous as she left the garden center and drove toward town. The thought of stopping at the market on the way home unexpectedly popped into her head. It had been months since she had entered those doors. Just after Fred's death she had gone there on a busy Saturday and had found herself waiting in line at the checkout. A major attack of panic had seized her there and it seemed a miracle that she had been able to escape from the place at all. So, she had not been able to go back. She reached the street where the market was located, and almost without her knowledge or approval her clenched hands turned the steering wheel to the left onto Green Street. The market was two blocks away. She pulled into the lot that ran along one side and parked the car. She sat there silently for a few moments breathing hard, and scanned her physical being and realized the tightness in her chest and back were signaling the panic to come. The thoughts of that earlier visit had come back to her in a rush. How would she ever find the courage to leave the car and go inside?

CHAPTER 8

Kath sat in the car and waited until a bit of calmness came back. Going to the market had once upon a time, in another life it seemed, been a pleasurable experience. Swallowing her fear and sudden dread she vowed she would do this. And finally, forcing a smile on her face, and ignoring the weakness in her hands and legs, she got out of the car and walked slowly around to the front of the store.

She took a cart from the row near the front and went inside through the automatic door. Having the cart to push kept her steady as the atmosphere of the place instantly surrounded her. The smells of ground coffee and something baking were pungent but pleasant as she slowly moved inside. The market was busy. There seemed to be carts and customers in every aisle, and from somewhere there were the sounds of a baby crying. Just as she moved into one of the aisles, a child, a boy of about five, ran past her screaming followed by a woman with an overloaded cart, obviously his mother. The boy had rubbed against her, pushing her into a shelf and the woman's cart had jammed into hers. The rude woman just kept going, ignoring the fact that Kath had nearly been knocked over.

Things calmed a bit after that and Kath became aware that there was calming music playing in the background. She was able to pay attention to the shelves and began selecting a few items, milk, bread, the usual staples, some fruit, apples, grapes, and from the meat department hamburger and some chicken. She took a few moments in the pet department where she chose some canned food for Cassandra along with a package of tennis balls and a small stuffed animal which she assumed was a bear. Her final stop was the bakery department and she chose some cookies and a few donuts so that she would have something to offer Marcus if he showed up later. And she stopped there nearly frozen to the spot thinking of how these two individuals had entered her life, boy and dog, and had changed everything. She was standing there deep in thought when someone stopped by her cart and a booming voice cried, "Mrs. Longley, is it really you?"

She turned startled and found Henry Miller, the owner of the market standing next to her. He was obviously headed for his office which was located just beyond the bakery. Mr. Miller was a heavyset man, with a florid face who always seemed out of breath. He was usually in a hurry, but quite friendly. Today he was dressed in his usual white shirt and tie, and as always wore a green apron with the store logo Miller's Market printed at the top.

"Yes, it's me, Mr. Miller. I'm back. It's good to see you again."

"I've missed you, my dear. I understand you haven't been well. How are you coming along?"

"Much better. I'm doing okay. Thanks to your delivery service I've survived."

"Oh, we're so glad we've been able to keep that part of the business going. There are a lot of sick folks and shut ins who need us."

There was more small talk after that and just as Kath moved toward the check out and Mr. Miller was about to step into his office, he placed his hand on her arm and looked at her with a wide grin. He was a man who always enjoyed joking around and gossiping. "By the way, Mrs. Lonely. Your friend was in here a few days ago and I asked if she had seen you lately."

Kath knew at once who he was speaking of. He had called her Mrs. Lonely and she knew it was Geraldine Harvey.

"You didn't," Kath said. "You shouldn't have. You know she hates me."

"Yes, I'm well aware of that," Mr. Miller said. "She went into a long rant about how you are so stuck up! You think you know everything. You act like you are better than everybody in town."

Kath knew Mr. Miller enjoyed keeping the feud going between the two of them. In the past he had always told her the same things every chance he got.

"Why do you think she hates me so much, seriously, Mr. Miller," Kath asked, feeling a bit low. "And you shouldn't keep egging her on."

"She's touched, Mrs. Longley," He said then seriously, obviously sensing Kath was a bit irritated by his teasing. "You know she hates half the people in town, especially women, particularly women like you who have careers and are educated. She puts up with me because I help her a bit and give her breaks when things get rough. Don't let her get to you. See the humor in things as I do."

Humor. It seemed to Kath there was a thin line between humor and cruelty. Once Mr. Miller had gone into his office and closed the door, she moved slowly toward the checkout remembering what Jennifer Winston had told her earlier about confrontation without anger. Perhaps she hadn't enough strength to do it now, today, but she knew one day before long she would have it, and she would confront Geraldine Harvey regardless of what the consequences would be. She had done nothing that should have caused her anger toward her except for the day that she walked to the store and stopped at Mrs. Harvey's porch where she was sitting as she usually did, enjoying the sun. Kath was only trying to be friendly when she spoke a warm Hello and stopped at a flower bed below the porch and pulled a weed. It was obvious to her at the time that Mrs. Harvey didn't know the difference between a weed and a flower. "Why did you do that!" The woman had raged. "It was a weed," Kath had told her. "I was trying to be helpful." "It was beautiful," Geraldine Harvey had spat. "It was beautiful." And then she had burst into tears. Kath had apologized but nothing could have mattered to the woman at that moment, and ever after she had roamed the neighborhood telling everyone who would listen, "Old Mrs. Lonely knows everything!"

Luckily there was no long line at the checkout when she got there. For once there were three lanes open and she slipped into one where the checkout girl was putting the last item into a plastic bag and then into a lady's cart.

The girl was so fast once the belt moved and Kath's items were in front of her that there was no time for anxiety or a panic attack. It was all she could do to get the bank card from her purse and then into the proper slot. She was out of the store, standing in the sunlight once again, before she realized she hadn't said thank you to the girl who had placed her bags into her cart and smiled at her warmly.

Kath headed toward home feeling quite weary and a bit anxious. She was happy for what she had accomplished that afternoon but concerned that Cassandra had been alone in her cage for a long period of time. She had shut the door for once before she left for the doctor's, and she was sure the dog would now be ready to go outside. Parking in the driveway opposite the back door, she grabbed a bag of groceries from the back seat and her purse and headed toward the house when Marcus suddenly appeared, walking quickly up from Park Street, across the yard to where she stood. He was wearing shorts and a tee shirt, one that was stained and whatever logo had been printed on it was now only a smudge of color.

"I was worried about you," he said quickly. "I came by earlier and Cassandra barked from inside. I thought something might have happened."

"I just had to go to the doctor," Kath said, opening the door. "I stopped at the garden center and the market." From inside Cassandra was barking excitedly. "Could you please go to her and then bring her outside for a run? Afterwards you can help get my things from the car."

A short time later Kath went out and headed toward the car again. It was nearly evening by this time and the air was warm and alive with sounds from uptown, the usual sounds of cars moving and horns blowing. But from behind the house and up the long slope, the park lay in shadows. The sky above was streaked with white luminous clouds. Off to the left the sun was setting behind the trees leaving a wide golden track that nearly stopped her heart. It had been months since she had really been able to stop and see what was happening in the natural world. She loved nature, the birds and the growing things. It gave her a feeling of reserved joy knowing she was headed in the right direction, returning to the woman she had once been. But was one ever able to go home again? You could, she realized. But nothing would ever be as it once was. Fred was gone, there was missing time. She felt years older. The flower pots were empty...

"Your grass needs mowed," Marcus said, bringing her back from her reverie. "Do you want me to do it now?" He was standing at the edge of the patio, Cassandra on her leash looking up at him.

"It can wait until tomorrow," Kath told him. "Just take Cassandra inside and you can help me carry in the things I bought."

There was a brief pause as they stood there, Kath staring off at the park, when a faded green pickup truck came to a screeching stop opposite them on Park Street. Glancing in the direction of the truck she saw the driver leaning across the seat gesturing wildly. He was yelling at them, but the sounds of the engine were so loud she couldn't make out what he was saying. She caught the words, "Get home, now!"

"It's my Dad," Marcus said, his face a mixture of fear and defiance. Just as he said it, the truck moved quickly away and was off up Park street in a cloud of smoke.

"Don't you think you should go home then," she asked, feeling rather low. She wasn't prepared for another confrontation with the man at this moment.

"No!" Marcus said angrily. "I know he doesn't want

me being friendly with you, or anyone for that matter. He's afraid I might tell you his secrets, my suspicions..."

Marcus stopped there and took Cassandra into the house. When he came back Kath led him to the car and they carried in the remaining bags of groceries and the geraniums from the trunk. Kath sat the plants next to the empty pots on the patio and went back into the house, Marcus following. Kath made a cup of coffee and offered Marcus a coke, which he took in a shaking hand, she noticed. Then they sat down at the kitchen table.

"What is it your father doesn't want you to tell me," Kath asked, stirring her coffee.

Marcus lowered his eyes appearing to be caught off guard. "Oh, I don't know what his problem is," He finally blurted. "He has a thousand excuses why he doesn't want me being friendly with you."

"But you mentioned secrets, suspicions," Kath said, not letting him off the hook. "What did you mean?"

Marcus was silent for a moment and then he spoke in a soft voice. "Well my mother told me once that he was in a lot of trouble when he was a teenager."

"What kind of trouble," Kath asked when Marcus sat silently, a bit too long.

"There was a party... And my father and a friend were playing with a gun. Or so my father said. They were alone in a room and his friend ended up dead."

"Oh my," Kath blurted. "How awful. What happened."

"It was a big thing at the time. My father went to trial for murder. Some of the boy's friends said they had been angry with each other. They were involved in something bad. Drugs, burglary. No one knew. They said Dad killed him to keep it quiet."

"But what happened then," Kath asked, breath-lessly. Even the thought of what Marcus was telling her caused her anxiety and panic to close in on her.

"Dad got on the stand and told them that he had had the gun in his hands but had laid it down on the table. He said his friend picked it up and the gun went off. The jury found Dad not guilty because the gun was near the boy's hand."

"What did your mother think? Did she know your father then?"

"She knew of him," Marcus said, looking down at the table and twisting his can of coke. "It was a couple of years later before they got together. By that time the whole thing had faded, but people, at least some peo-ple, still believed he was guilty."

"And your mother?"

"She believed his story at the time," Marcus told her. "But years later when I was about seven, she told me something that made me wonder. Dad had started drinking heavily and had hit her one night when he came home all drunk and everything. She believed he had been chasing another woman and there were ru-mors he had roughed up a girl in a bar. He has a vi-olent temper, she told me. "He killed once, and he'll kill again!" Marcus stopped suddenly, placing his hand over his mouth where his face had taken on a twisted look.

"Do you think she really believed that or was she just angry?"

Marcus didn't answer her at once but just sat there shaking his head. "Sometimes when he was hard on her she seemed to hate him," Marcus said after a pause. "But other times when he was half decent, she seemed to dote on him and he could do no wrong. It might have been one of those times when she hated him that she said what she did..."

"And what about you Marcus," Kath asked. "What do you think?"

"I don't know. I get all mixed up inside. I mean I try to get along with him," Marcus said, a catch in his voice. "I used to care about him; but he's gotten worse as time goes on. When I'm old enough I'll get away from him, because the truth is, I hate him now. He drove my mother away and he beats up on me. And sometimes I think he did kill his friend. I think he got away with murder!"

It was dark by the time Marcus left her. She dreaded the thought of him having to go back home and was fearful of what might be waiting for him there. And as she closed and locked the back door after her young friend left, Kath felt fear wash over her as well. His last words to her had sent a pang of terror through her. Marcus's mother had told him he would kill again. Was Marcus in real danger? Was she? She went through the house and checked all the locks, half expecting Marcus's father would return and break into the house and do her harm. She suddenly felt vulnerable, and even Cassandra seemed to sense that something might be wrong. Could dogs really pick up on what their humans were feeling? In any case, the animal followed her around the rest of the evening and even seemed to want to climb the stairs with her at bedtime and stood below in the hallway for a few moments before returning to the living room and her cage. Kath was sure she would alert her if anyone tried entering the house in the night. It was amazing to Kath how much the dog had come out of her shell since

Marcus had rescued her from certain death. He was the one who had brought her back to life again. Love and caring had done the trick.

It was a few days later when the surveyor, a Mr. Gillan, came to check on the boundary of her property. He was a friendly sort of guy and chuckled when Kath told him of her feud with her neighbor. "I hear this all the time," he said. "Most of my business comes to me due to men like that who are afraid someone is trying to steal a few inches of ground from them, or a few feet. It doesn't matter."

He did the survey quickly. Kath stood for a few moments on the patio and watched while he carefully measured her property at the rear next to the park and of course the property line between the two driveways. The fact that he was doing a survey was not unnoticed by Mr. Kline. Kath glanced in that direction from time to time and saw the movement of the window curtains. Kline himself came out of the house and stood at the edge of the driveway for a few moments glaring at them. Kath stared back at him, but then turned away and focused on the geraniums that Marcus had helped her plant in the pots a couple of days before. He had also brought the folding chairs from the garage and Kath sat down in one and while the surveyor did his work she focused on the beauty of the park beyond her yard. It was May now and all the trees were in leaf. The scents coming to her as she sat there were exquisite, essences of the earth and of time and memory. Somewhere behind her in the winter dark, caught and held by her addiction, she had wanted to die. Now it was spring and more than ever she felt the stirrings of a new season within herself.

A few days later the fence people arrived. The surveyor had placed wooden stakes between the driveways and across the back of the yard. "Those are the correct boundaries of your property," Mr. Gillan had told her. "Give the old man four or five inches. He won't be able to cause you any trouble."

But the fence men had no sooner begun the digging of the holes for the posts that would support the fence when a police car drove slowly up Park Street and parked next to her yard. A tired appearing officer emerged from the car and strolled across the lawn toward where Kath was sitting on the patio watching the progress.

"I'm Officer Braden," he said. "We had a call from your neighbor over here that you are digging holes in his yard."

Just as the officer walked up, Kath caught a glimpse of Mr. Kline coming out of his house and walking to the middle of his driveway. Once again, he stood there glaring at her. Kath stood up casually and introduced herself to the officer. "I think he's mistaken, Officer Braden," she said. "I am simply building a fence." She walked to the edge of her yard and stood only feet from Kline. The officer followed. She wanted to be sure he could hear every word she said. "I just had my yard surveyed a few days ago," she went on. "The stakes in the ground are the property line. The fence will go up a few inches beyond that in my direction."

"There digging up my property," Kline spoke suddenly his voice shrill. Even the officer seemed taken aback. "Why there's never been a fence here, never!"

"No, you are right," Kath said, walking even closer to where Kline stood, making sure her feet were planted firmly on her own driveway. She spoke quietly and didn't raise her voice one decibel. "There has never been a fence here, and there would never have been one, Mr. Kline, if you had been a decent neighbor to me as you once were to my husband. You obviously have a major problem with women."

"I'll have my attorney look into this," he yelled. "I'll bring a law suit!"

"Bring it on, Mr. Kline," Kath said, voice still lowered in the same non-confrontational tone. "And if I see you slinking anywhere near my property, I'll bring a lawsuit myself, one for stalking and harassment. You are a despicable neighbor, Mr. Kline. You should be ashamed of the way you've treated me. And you should be happy I'm giving you a beautiful wooden wall to stare at when you look out your window. And before the fence goes up, the bags of leaves you placed behind my garage, along with the tree limbs, will be put back on your property. So, when you see this happening, don't bother to call the police. You'll be sorry if you do!"

She must have shocked Kline to the core, for he didn't utter another word. As Kath turned to walk away the officer moved toward where Kline was standing, and as she went in to the house she turned and saw him talking to the officer, his hands gesturing wildly.

As she sat down later with a cup of coffee, she couldn't believe the audacity of Kline to call the police about her building a fence. But it gave her a certain sense of satisfaction that she had stood up to him. She supposed that it had helped her release some of the anger she felt toward her neighbor, but it wasn't that simple. It was a practice that would become easier with time, yet she still wished with all her heart that Fred was still alive to stand next to her at times like this.

Once the fence was completed it looked quite attractive, Kath felt. It surrounded her property beautifully but also turned out to be quite useful. Above all, the chain link part which surrounded the yard and garden itself made a lovely enclosure that would keep Cassandra safe, and she could go out to the grass without a leash. And it especially would not shield her from looking at the beauty of the park behind her property. Kath felt a certain sense of safety and security herself now that it was in place. She could walk out and enjoy the sun and the weather without feeling Kline's eyes staring at her.

Marcus thought the fence was a good thing as well. He could romp with Cassandra there since it was quite a large space, and he began to throw tennis balls to her which she learned easily what was expected of her and returned them time and time again. The look she wore on her face when she returned the balls and lay them at Marcus's feet was one of happiness and pure joy.

Kath would sit on the patio and watch them play and would try to feel joyful herself, but in the background was the vague feelings of anxiety that seemed always to be present. Occasionally there would be moments and periods of time where she forgot her feelings but then the slightest thought would surface and remind her, they were still there, just short of the panic that accompanied them.

And of course, she would worry about Marcus and his father. If his father wanted to keep the boy at home, Marcus continued to show up at her door like clockwork. She was never sure when he would come, it might be morning or evening and sometimes both, but he was always there to help her where she needed. He mowed the grass and kept the yard shipshape, he helped with dishes when she insisted he have a meal with her. And of course, he took care of Cassandra, taking her for walks, or brushing her coat which had grown long and unruly. When the dog first came, she was jumpy and the slightest movement would cause her to be afraid, but with Marcus's caring she had settled into a happier and more easy disposition. Kath assured him they would take her to be groomed soon. When she asked Marcus what had happened when he went home the night his father had pulled up alongside the yard and yelled at him to come home, he told her that when he slipped into the house that night his Dad was passed out on the sofa.

On a bright May morning soon after the fence was put into place, Kath was having coffee on the patio with Cassandra at her feet when Marcus showed up, causing Cassandra to burst into a series of friendly barks. He came through the side gate and she rushed to him, standing on her hind legs to greet him.

Marcus, as usual was dressed in shorts and a faded tee shirt that literally hung on him, the front covered by faded blobs of color. Once he was settled into the other chair, Kath suggested he should buy some new tee shirts with the money she had been giving him for the work he was doing for her.

Oh, I don't need any new things," Mrs. Longley. "I'm okay with what I have."

"But what do with the money I give you? You said you wanted a new pair of shoes, but I see the same ones on your feet that you've always wore."

"I'm saving it, Mrs. Longley," Marcus said, putting all his attention on the dog who was sitting at his feet waving her tail.

"But what are you saving it for," Kath asked. But Marcus just shook his head and suddenly stood up.

"I think she wants to go for a walk, Mrs. Longley!" He said. "Do you mind if I take her into the Park? I'll get her leash."

The thought of walking in the park again had frightened her up to that point, but when Marcus came out of the house and fastened the leash to the dog's collar, she stood up. "I think I'll go with you this morning," she said excitedly, covering the hints of anxiety that were present, attempting to change her mind.

Marcus seemed happy she was going, but as they excited the side gate, Cassandra began pulling on the leash. "I hope you can keep up with us," he said. "She really walks fast."

"Maybe you should slow her down a bit," Kath warned. "I'm not so sure her hip has healed completely as yet."

But by the time they reached the first path into the park, Marcus and Cassandra were already a distance from her. "We'll stop somewhere and wait for you," he called back to her.

Kath took her time, walking at a regular pace trying to keep her anxiety at bay. It was such a splendid morning and the sights of the park ahead of her were breathtaking. It was a green world and the breeze was warm on her face. They park was beautifully kept and the scent of freshly cut grass was all around her. Off in the distance Marcus and Cassandra were already halfway up the first hill and there were no other humans that she could see anywhere. The park paths had been paved with macadam, so the walking was easy. She was wearing slacks and a blouse and the shoes on her feet were light and quite comfortable. The path crossed the park and then turned sharply and climbed a long hill next to a wood. The sun had shone brightly on her face so far, but on the uphill section there was shade and shadow. In the woods there were the sounds of birds and insects, and an occasional squirrel scampered here and there as she walked. The sights and sounds of nature never failed to calm her spirits.

At the top of the first hill she sat down on a comfortable bench for a moment, breathing deeply. The park was equipped with numerous benches, and sitting on this one she could see her house and the town in the distance. Directly in front of her and down the slope was a large baseball diamond. The local high school team used it for there games and when they were playing was the only time very many people walked there. Scanning the park as it lay above and below her, she could see no sign of Marcus and Cassandra. For a moment she felt as though she were alone in the world, far from all the worries and problems that had recently assailed her.

At the top of the hill the path led out into the sun once again, and then up another hill and another which was quite steep and left her breathless. For the first time she felt warm and uncomfortable. Reaching the top of the last hill she stopped for a moment and looked back. The world lay below her. Now she could see three distant figures near a pavilion at the edge of the baseball diamond, but they seemed far away. Her problems too, lay at some distant place, along with her anxiety. But she was sure she would catch up with it again before long.

The path split at that point, one arm leading downward toward the park entrance, allowing one to escape from the walk in an easier and quicker direction. Since she saw no sight of Marcus and Cassandra in that direction, she took the upper path. This section continued to climb upward, though in an easier slant. It led through a field of large boulders and twisted its way to the top of the park. Here she was surrounded by deep woods and the sight of the path suddenly plunging downward gave her a feeling of sudden fear. She stopped for a moment before carefully making her way down, realizing that the fear had come from the thought that it was a bit dangerous for her to be alone there. Any person or thing could come from the woods at any moment to confront her.

She hurried her pace but still had to step carefully. The path was quite steep and as she made her way downward with the greatest caution, she caught the scent of something dead down the slope to her left. There was the faint sound of insects buzzing. Something had died and the thought of an animal somewhere in the underbrush being feasted on by other forest creatures was almost more than she could bear.

She picked up her pace and finally made it to the bottom of the slope, her heart beating out of control in her chest. But she moved forward as calmly as possible and before long caught the sight of movement through the green in front of her. Not far away she caught sight of another bench and saw that Marcus and Cassandra were waiting for her there.

She had calmed quite a bit by the time she reached

them. Cassandra was happy to see her and stood on her hind legs and licked Kath's fingers as she held her hand toward her. "Better sit down and rest for a while, Mrs. Longley," Marcus said, smiling. "That's a rough climb isn't it? Maybe we should have taken the shorter path."

"It's a bit late to think of that now," Kath said, sitting down on the bench and trying to breath easier. She was having a hard time getting the smell of the dead animal out of her mind. Off in front of her she saw the very high chain link fence that separated the park from the land owned by the railroad. From there she could see that the path turned sharply to the left and followed the fence all the way back to Park Street and the park entrance. Somewhere in the thick woods behind the fence was the camp the boys from town had made that Marcus had told her about. As they sat there the loud sound of a train passing on the tracks beyond caused her to realize how close they were to the place.

"Is that where the boys have their camp," Kath asked, once her breathing had slowed and she had recovered from the hard walk.

"Yes," Marcus answered, pointing toward the woods, his face showing traces of concern. "It's back there a way beyond the trees. There are paths that go in that direction, but you must go through thicket to get there. It's like a maze."

"Is there just one way in," Kath asked, suddenly feeling quite tense again.

"The best way is down from the railroad tracks," Marcus told her. That's the way the boys get in there. They climb up the hill just beyond the big bridge and then down from the tracks. I can get in from across Park street from where we live. There's a narrow space where the fence runs into the embankment and a faint path that leads back. And if you look this way you can see where the fence ends here just a few yards from here."

Kath looked in the direction he was pointing and saw that the fence did end not far from where they sat. There was a patch of weeds and wild bushes that began where the path turned, but she could see that the greenery had been trampled slightly toward the end of the fence forming a crude path.

"Someone must have gone back there," Kath said, pointing to the faint trail.

"If they go near the camp the boys will run them off," Marcus said. "Just like they do me if I go back."

"Don't you go back there again," Kath warned. "Sounds like it could be dangerous!"

"I'm not scared!" Marcus stood up defiantly. "Besides I am going to go back again. I'm going to find out if they might have stolen the furniture from your porch."

This was not the first time Marcus had mentioned that the gang of boys might have stolen the things from her porch. When she had first told him the furniture was missing, he had suggested they might be the guilty party and now he had brought it up again.

"It doesn't matter about the things that were stolen." Kath said quickly. "There's no reason for your going back there again! Besides, I'm sure it was Kline who stole it. He probably has my furniture in his garage!"

Marcus was silent then, eyes peering toward the woods, his face taut. Kath finally stood up and told him they should get started back. Once again Marcus and Cassandra led the way as they followed the path along the fence toward Park Street. There was a stark difference between the smooth looking Park to her left beyond a narrow strip of trees, and the dark jungle-like growth that lay on the other side of the fence. Nature had already encroached on the Park as new trees had grown up through the fence at intervals only to have been snipped off by the park maintenance people. Outcroppings of rock jutted against the fence at several places, giving her the feeling that what lay beyond the fence was a prison.

Kath was warm again by this time and stopped to wipe her face with her hands. Small insects, gnats she supposed, were buzzing around her face. Noticing she had stopped, Marcus came back to where she was standing. "We need to cut across the park here and get back to your house on the other side. It's all grass and we'll cut through by the baseball field. I don't want my Dad to see us. He has binoculars and sometimes he sits in there and stares out at the park. He says he's bird-watching, but I think he's looking at people, at women probably. I just don't want him giving you a hard time."

Just as they were about to turn in the direction of the park itself, Cassandra pulled at her leash, drawn by something that was half lying in a patch of weeds by the side of the path next to the fence. Marcus stopped while the dog sniffed at what she had found. Kath moved closer to have a look. It was a pink tee shirt all bundled together and a single tennis shoe, laced with a pink shoe lace lay next to it.

Somehow Kath suddenly felt a sharp wave of anxiety and she stared downward. It was strange to see the objects there in such an out of the way spot, so out of place. She suddenly stared at Marcus and saw that he too, had been startled by their finding the objects along the path. His mouth was open in surprise as he pulled Cassandra away. Without a work he turned sharply and headed in the direction of the park itself. Kath followed feeling a bit weak and faint. It was her anxiety, she told herself. It was the single shoe that had startled her so. The things had probably dropped out of someone's bag as they were walking. There was a simple explanation. But what about Marcus? He had been startled by the discovery as well. And just now he was walking faster than ever, and Kath was not sure if it was his or her heavy breathing she heard as they hurried away.

CHAPTER 9

By the time they were back at the house Kath was breathing normally again. The walk in the park had exhausted her and Marcus seemed just as tired and soon said he would have to go home. His father had needed his help, he said, and if he didn't show up, he would punish him in some way.

Kath went upstairs and lay across the bed for what she thought would be a short rest. Her anxiety was changing, she realized, as she lay there, the light breeze from the open window touching her face. The medication she was taking was obviously helping. The attacks of panic she had experienced in the past, the ones that came on with all their power to fell her, had changed now into short spurts, that came quickly with little or no provocation and left just as quickly. It had been that way when they came across the lost shoe and tee shirt in the park. She had felt a sudden burst of panic, but it had soon lifted. She fell asleep after going over everything in her mind, and when she awoke much later, her only thought was on going downstairs and seeing if Cassandra was alright.

It wasn't until several days later that she thought of the incident again. It was June now, Spring was morphing into summer. Everywhere she looked there were mixed hues of colors. Flowers in beds and pots lay around every corner, misting her eyes. She had taken to driving to the store on a weekly basis. She could do that far more comfortably now. She needed to get used to going places without being afraid of making the effort. The drive to the market that morning was uneventful, she was feeling upbeat and was thinking of what she would buy for dinner that evening. She had been thinking of a salad and perhaps a steak. It was summer after all and she needed some drinks, soda and tea.

Walking into the market a stand with a stack of the local paper caught her eye. LOCAL GIRL MISSING!" Kath reached down and picked one up. She started to read the story but a woman behind her coughed loudly, and she realized she was blocking the door. Apologizing profusely, she moved into the main aisle of the store. She thought of picking up the paper and reading more but it would be too conspicuous and rude of her to block any shelf or aisle in the place. At the check-out at last the girl who picked up the paper to scan it, held it for a few brief seconds and gasped. "Marjorie Winters," she cried. "I knew her from school! Missing for two weeks?" The girl was silent then and just stared at Kath wide eyed. She was very helpful and loaded Kath's bags into the cart. "I hope they find her," was all she said as Kath wheeled her cart toward the door.

Seeing the headlines just as she entered the store, had set off a kind of chain reaction in Kath. One thought after another, one bit more of tension, another twist of her imagination, had Kath in an early mode of panic by the time her things had been put away and she was able to sit at the table and read the story about the missing girl. She had gone to a baseball game in the park, her parents reported. She was to meet some friends there and would be home as soon as the game was finished. But none of her friends had met her there and had assumed she had changed her plans at the last minute and hadn't even gone to the park.

Or had she? The sudden picture of the lone shoe and the tee shirt she and Marcus had found in the park sent a wave of fear rushing through her. Could that have anything do with the missing girl? She shook her head and breathed deeply. It was only a bad thought in a tired mind. The book she had read about Anxiety and Depression had warned about how easily such a thing could happen and quite easily become an obsession.

When Marcus showed up later that afternoon, slipping into the house quietly by the back door as he usually did, Kath showed him the paper. She said nothing to him as he slowly read the story, wondering if he too, might associate the missing girl with the objects they had found in the park. He read with much interest, holding the paper close to his head as though he had problems with his vision. His face was taut and his eyes wide when he was finished and laid the paper down.

"You don't suppose that has anything to do with the shoe we found that day," he said, his voice quite serious.

"I was wondering the same thing," Kath told him. "The whole thing has given me chills. I wonder if we should have taken the shoe and the shirt to the maintenance people in the park that day?"

"Someone probably already did, Mrs. Longley." Marcus told her. "Besides we can't jump to conclusions like that."

"But I felt fearful that day when I saw the things

lying there. It was the idea of only the one shoe that did it. Imagination can be a bad thing."

"Yes," Marcus said quietly. "Sometimes it makes you wonder if what you saw or heard was real."

"What do you mean," Kath asked, folding the paper and rubbing her hands together to stop them from shaking.

But Marcus shook his head and said no more. Instead he grabbed Cassandra's leash from the hook and took her outside for a run. The dog had come to lay by his feet the moment he entered the house as she always did, and with whimpering and little nudges had asked to be taken outside. The boy always obliged her.

When he returned to the house with the dog, Marcus seemed quite serious and subdued. The usually upbeat, smiling boy was gone and in his place a far more tight-lipped person who appeared to be deep in thought, having moved inside himself to a place that Kath could not reach.

After he was gone that afternoon, Kath sat wondering what in the world could have caused the obvious change in his spirits. Had their talk of the missing girl gotten to him causing him to feel a primal sense of fear, or was it his relationship with a father who treated him badly with abuse and punishment that had brought the switch?

In the morning Marcus didn't come as he usually did. Kath waited to see if he might appear to take Cassandra outside for a morning walk and when he didn't show up, she attached Cassandra's leash and took her outside herself. It was a perfect morning. The sun shone from a flawless sky and the breeze was gentle and carried all the fresh scents of summer down the hill from the park. Kath had not gone back there since the day she and Marcus had walked there together, and although she had no desire to walk to the far side where the fence and the woods had caused such fear to rise in her, she decided she and Cassandra would walk along the closer side, where the path led up the first long hill, next to the woods. The exercise had obviously helped her that day to feel stronger, and Jennifer Winston, who she would be seeing again soon, had told her she should exercise to help heal the anxiety. Cassandra had obviously walked the path many times with Marcus and she led the way now, walking quickly, almost too quickly, Kath felt. The dog walked straight ahead, seldom turning her head to the thicket across from the path where there was the sound of birds and small animals scampering, and the incessant whirring of insect wings.

At the top of the hill Kath gently tugged the animal to a stop and sat down on the familiar bench. Below her the park with the baseball field lay in a cocoon of summer haze, green and sunlit, almost other worldly. And further in the distance was the deeper woods, protected on one side by the railroad and on the other by the chain link fence and the path along which Cassandra had discovered the shoe and shirt. She doubted she would ever walk there again.

She was sitting there deep in thought, her eyes on the summer scene below when Cassandra let out a loud bark, her attention drawn to the path they had just climbed. A man was walking swiftly in her direction, Kath noticed. At first, she didn't recognize him and turned her eyes away believing him to be a stranger. But when the man was directly opposite her, he stopped, and Kath recognized him at once. It was James Gordon, her neighbor who lived opposite her, across Park Street and up on the hill. He must be over sixty now, she realized. His hair was nearly all gray and his face had deeper lines than she remembered.

"Kath," Mr. Gordon said, holding out his hand to her. "I haven't seen you for months. I think the last time I spoke to you was at Fred's viewing."

There was silence for a moment. James Gordon had obviously realized he had opened a forbidden door. Kath sat quite still for a moment remembering. Many people had come to the funeral home that night to pay their respects to Fred. Most of them she didn't know as they were people who had worked with him at the fire station. She closed her eyes trying to remember speaking to Mr. Gordon that night, but her mind was blank. When she opened them, the gentleman was staring down at her, a worried look on his face.

"Are you okay, Kath," he asked.

"Oh yes, James, I was just trying to remember that night. There were so many people..."

"Yes, Fred was well thought of by a lot of folks."

"Why don't you sit a moment," Kath said, noticing he was fidgeting a bit and had just leaned down to pat Cassandra on her head.

"Thank you," he said. "I think I will for a moment. Walking up that hill is a bit tiring."

"Do you come here often?"

"I try to walk every day," he said, grinning. "But only on the easy side. Those upper hills are a little steep I'm afraid."

As James Gordon sank down on the opposite end of the bench, Kath thought back to the early days

when she and Fred had first moved to the neighborhood. They had become casual friends of the
Gordons. Teresa, James's wife had been a friendly
woman, quite neighborly, and had arranged several
occasions for them to spend time together. There had
been dinners and card games. And then Teresa had
been involved in a terrible accident one night coming home in the snow and had been a cripple until
her death.

"How long has it been since Teresa died," Kath
asked, looking across to where James sat, patting
Cassandra's head.

"Oh, it must be fifteen years now," He said. "I don't
keep track anymore. Life goes on and I just go along for
the ride."

"Grief is hard, isn't it," Kath said, lowering her eyes.
"It's been difficult for me. I'm just now beginning to
feel normal again."

"It will get better," James said. "Time is a strange
thing. It makes us older but better in many ways."

He stood up and looked back the way he had come.
"Why haven't you called me," he suddenly asked nervously, shuffling his feet. "The night of Fred's viewing I
asked you to call if you needed anything. When I didn't
hear from you, I just assumed you wanted to be left
alone. When we had the big storm, I came down to see
if you might need some help, but I saw someone had
shoveled you out."

"Oh, I'm sorry, James." Kath said. "So much was
going on that night. I don't even remember talking to
you. I was around the bend for a long time. But thank
you for telling me that."

She stood up and shook his hand. "I'm sorry we have

the hill between us," she went on. "We live so close and yet so far. I forget there's a house up there."

"Yes, but there is a path as well," he said. "Walk up it some time, and call if you need anything."

James Gordon shook her hand and walked away quickly. She watched as he continued up the hill, a tall man walking swiftly into the sunlight.

Kath suddenly felt a bit ashamed. She had been lost in her own awful place and had nearly drank herself into oblivion. Help had been so close, and she had not reached out for it. But she had been so lucky to find Marcus. Perhaps that was the way it was supposed to be.

Kath finally got up from the bench and continued her walk. James Gordon had disappeared by this time, but she couldn't get him off her mind. She wondered how he had coped after his wife's death. And had he ever tried to find another woman to share his life. Perhaps he hadn't even been lonely. She hoped she would be able to hear his story some time and share with him a bit more of hers.

On her return visit to Jennifer Winston a few days later, Kath brought up the subject of James Gordon. The counselor had asked her if she was getting out a bit more and if she was trying to connect with people, and she mentioned meeting her friend in the park.

"Why in the world do you think I kept myself from reaching out to him," she asked. "He obviously would have helped me in some way. It would have been a comfort to me, I'm sure."

"Don't look to deeply for those kinds of answers," Jennifer Winston told her. "You are slowly working your way out of a dark place. The light around you will get brighter as you go. We very often find out that the help we were seeking was closer than we realized."

Yes, I know that now," Kath told her. "But at the time I wanted to hide, to isolate myself."

"And have you worked on letting go of your anger," Mrs. Winston asked. "Remember we discussed that the last time you were here."

"I stood up to my neighbor," Kath told her. "I had the fence built between our driveways and around my property."

"And how did that make you feel?"

"Better, much better."

While Kath continued to feel as though she were turning toward the light again, she was a bit concerned that Marcus was moving backward. Ever since the morning the two of them had discussed the missing girl, he had seemed to be preoccupied and sullen. He would come and take care of the chores she had for him, and take Cassandra outside for play or walks, but when he sat with her at the table afterward, he would sit staring down at his hands and have little to say.

It was on a morning in early July that Kath had a talk with him to question why he was behaving in such a worrisome manner.

"What's going on, Marcus." She said. "You don't seem yourself lately." She had made him an egg sandwich for breakfast, but he hadn't touched it. Even his coffee, of which he was fond, had not been touched.

"I guess it's my Dad," Marcus said, finally. He didn't look at her directly but kept his attention on Cassandra who was sitting at his feet as she usually did.

"Is he being aggressive? What?" Kath asked. "We

can go to the authorities, you know. If you can't handle it any longer, we can do something. I'll take you there..."

"No!" Marcus said emphatically. "They would put me somewhere, with strangers. He threatens me with that all the time. He hates me coming here and says if I don't stop, he'll turn me over to Children and Youth! Somehow, he is afraid of you. I tell him you are good and kind, but he always turns it around and makes it bad..."

"Do you want me to go and face him, have a talk with him," Kath asked. "I will you know. This is crazy!"

"Yes, I know and it's making me crazy, too," Marcus said, standing up. "I can't sleep and I'm having nightmares!"

"Oh my, Marcus, I'm sorry," Kath said. "What kind of nightmares?"

"Just scary things," he said lowering his voice. "It's over and over, I'm in the woods in the dark. There's a light and someone is being chased."

"Is it you, Marcus?" Kath asked softly. "Are you being chased?"

"Oh, I don't know," he said, shaking his head. "It may be that girl who's missing!"

He grabbed Cassandra's leash and he and the dog were out the door before she had a chance to question him further. Kath sat there for what seemed a long time trying to make some sense of what Marcus had said. The idea of the missing girl had obvious not set well with him. And how in the world could he go on dealing with such a hateful father? But other than being kind and supportive, there was little she could do to make him feel better. Even though she had been giving him money regularly for helping her with the yard and so on, the boy was still wearing the same ratty looking shorts and tee shirts. She didn't like to ask him what he was doing with the money. He had told her on several occasions that he was saving it. Originally, he had said he was saving to buy new shoes, but he hadn't done that either. Perhaps she could offer to take him to the department store down at the shopping center, or even to the mall in Clarksburg. Better still, the next time she was out she would buy him some things. He had told her he would be fourteen in July, so it could be a birthday gift. Surely, he would not object to that.

After returning with Cassandra from the morning walk, Marcus disappeared as quickly as he had come. Kath finished her own morning chores and then sat upstairs in her office going through her papers and paying bills. She had taken to writing again in her journal. And this time she wrote about Marcus and how much he had helped her and how she worried about his welfare. She also wrote of the missing girl and running into James Gordon in the park. When the words stopped flowing, she sat concentrating for a moment on her own physical self. She scanned her body from top to bottom and where there was tension, she attempted to release it. The view out the window was exquisite. Her eyes were drawn to the far side of the street where the stream ran through a green jungle of trees. She could not see the water itself, but she loved the mists that seemed to rise from it and seeing the birds that rose and fell above the mist. The window was open to the screen and the scents of summer drifting in had her suddenly longing to be outside. The temperature was slightly warm, but a breeze was playing with the window curtain.

In a sudden flash she decided she would go outside

for a walk. But this time she would stay away from the park, and instead go up Bridge Street toward the town and end up veering along Green Street, to the market and back. She would take along a shopping bag in which she could carry a few items for she had no desire to overburden herself on the way back. Seeing that Cassandra was sleeping quietly in her cage, Kath left the house quickly by the front door, and stood for a moment drinking in the exquisite summer air before beginning her trek.

Bridge Street was lined with shade trees and walking along it was always pleasant. The street ran smoothly along until Anderson's Creek veered sharply to the right and began its journey south through the town. Then the street began to climb Anderson's Hill where when it reached the top, it moved into the main part of the town. Green Street where Miller's Market was located went off to the right just a short distance beyond.

The houses moved closer to each other where the street rose up and Kath found herself breathing deeply as she made the climb. Her anxiety stirred a bit as she walked, but by now, she could scan it without fear and by doing this it always seemed to move further away. It was along this stretch of street where Geraldine Harvey lived in her ramshackle house. It had been built of wood long before and the white paint of the exterior and the green of the fragile shutters had faded long ago. Vines grew along one side where a narrow side yard led to the back porch. Below the smaller front porch lay the notorious flower bed where Kath had pulled the weed and caused such a stir those years ago. Today, as she approached the house, she could see that the lady herself was sitting there in the same straight-backed chair she usually occupied.

Approaching the house, Kath made up her mind that she would speak to the lady no matter what. And she suddenly realized that this would be the perfect time for getting her anger out into the open. She would let her know, as calmly as she possibly could, just how much her gossip and bad words had affected her. But when she reached the house, she saw that Geraldine Harvey appeared to be asleep. She was so still that for a moment Kath thought something might have happened to her. But looking closely she was able to see the rise and fall of her breath. Her head of disheveled gray hair was lowered and there appeared to be a slight smile on her face. She was dressed in a faded blue dress and had a flowered bandana wrapped around her neck. Kath stopped on the sidewalk just below her and softly spoke the ladies name. When there was no sign that Geraldine Harvey had heard her, she spoke again.

"Mrs. Harvey, are you awake?"

Again, there was no movement from the sleeping lady on the porch and looking in both directions Kath decided to walk on, not wanting to attract attention to herself. She would stop on the way back. Hopefully the woman would be awake by then. She was a bit disappointed that the opportunity of getting her feelings out in the open hadn't happened as she had hoped. But perhaps later when she returned it would.

At the market Kath picked up a paper from the rack on the way in. Marjorie Winters was still missing. She had pulled her cart into a corner in the vegetable section, and with heads of lettuce on one side and mounds of green peppers on the other she spent a couple of moments reading the story on the bottom of the front page. The police felt that the girl was a runaway. The parents on the other hand felt something bad had happened. A number was given so that anyone who knew anything of her whereabouts or had any information at all, should call and let the authorities know. Once again, the thought nagged at her she should call and tell them of the shoe and the shirt she and Marcus had discovered in the park. But as before she rejected the thought. Someone who had been playing tennis in the park, or baseball, softball or whatever had simply dropped them from an overfilled bag.

Leaving the market later, Kath had a sinking feeling. Going back toward Bridge Street her shopping bag was a bit heavy and she realized she had filled it with too many items. Shopping when one was nervous or hungry was always a bad idea. Nearing Geraldine Harvey's house she realized that the porch was empty. The lady had obviously woken up and gone back inside. Kath slowed as she reached the house and hesitated there for a moment. She thought of going up on the porch and knocking on the door but rejected the idea. Her bag was heavy, and she needed to get home. Besides, how did she know the shock of seeing her standing on her porch wouldn't send Geraldine Harvey into a screaming tailspin? It would be better if she just went on about her business and let the eventual run in with the lady happen in its own time.

Back at the house Cassandra seemed unusually glad to see her. She circled around her in the kitchen until her things were put away, and with a glass of iced tea in her hand, Kath took the dog out to the patio. While Cassandra explored the yard, Kath settled down into a chair in the quiet coolness and tried to relax. Off in the distance there was the sound of cheering and she realized there must be a baseball game in progress. She had almost forgotten it was Saturday and there was usually a game then in the afternoon.

She was sitting there almost asleep when Marcus came hurrying through the gate causing Cassandra who had been lying quietly by Kath's side to run off in his direction barking excitedly. The dog had only seen him that morning, but she seemed so excited Marcus had to get down on his knees and allow her to plant kisses all over his face. It gave Kath such a feeling of joy to see the two of them react like that to each other.

"My Dad's gone off to one of his clubs," Marcus said. "I thought I could take Cassandra a walk up into the park. There's a game going on up there. I don't think there'll will be many people up on the hill."

Marcus had seemed a little more upbeat than he had been lately, and she happily watched as he and the dog excited the gate and headed up the street toward the park entrance. She went back inside and laid out some hamburger and rolls. She would make some cheese-burgers and perhaps Marcus would eat one when he returned with Cassandra. They could eat them outside on the patio table.

She lost track of time and was sitting at the kitch-en table shaping the burgers when Marcus, carrying Cassandra in his arms, came rushing in the door. His face was red and sweating and he was breathing hard.

"There's a man out there," he said excitedly. "He followed us down from the park. He was watching the game from one of the benches. He tried to take Cassandra. He says she's his dog!"

"He said what?" Kath was stunned and got up from the table at once. "Where is he?"

"He's probably outside by now. I was almost running, carrying Cassandra, and he was right behind me!"

Kath rushed out to the patio just as a strange man, with a stern looking, almost angry face, came rushing up to the gate. He was wearing a denim cap and was dressed in jeans and a dirty gray shirt. Marcus and Cassandra had followed her, and the dog immediately burst into a series of angry barks and low threatening growls. Kath had never seen her behave like that, and she quickly told Marcus to take her inside. But it was almost all Marcus to do to keep her from rushing toward the gate.

Kath as calmly as she could walked up to the gate where the man was standing. She appeared calm but underneath she was about to burst into a full-fledged panic attack.

"What seems to be the problem, Sir," she asked. "What can I help you with?"

"That dog," the man coughed. "She's mine."

"Why do you think she's yours," Kath asked. "Obviously she's mine. She's here in my yard."

"It's the ear," you see," he said excitedly. "Bent down like that. It's unusual for a Westie's ear to do that. I'd recognize my Bella anywhere. She got out of the kennel one night, the door was let open you see..."

"I really think you must be mistaken, Sir." Kath said, holding on to the gate to keep her hands from shaking. "You see ... my son, Marcus, found this dog nearly dead behind our garage. She was beaten and had a very serious hip injury. The vet wasn't sure she would survive the night. He took photos of her and turned it over to the police and the humane society. If they ever find out who did that to her, they are going to arrest the guilty party immediately."

The man was silent then, his eyes darting from side to side. He looked across to where Marcus was having a hard time keeping Cassandra still, then glanced back the way he had come. He opened his mouth to say something, then lowered his eyes for a moment before speaking.

"Well, maybe I've made a mistake," he finally said, swallowing hard. "Maybe it isn't my Bella." He nodded then, turned and hurried back the way he had come.

Kath was breathing hard by this time and had difficulty letting go of the gate. Marcus came over to her, after finally setting Cassandra down, and lay his hand on her shoulder.

Are you alright, Mrs. Longley," he asked? "That was quite a story you told him. How did you come up with that? Do you think he'll come back?"

"I doubt he'll come back," Kath told him, slowly making her way back to the chair with his help. "Yes, I lied a bit, but I could tell I scared him. He was the person who did that to her. And he won't ever have the opportunity to do it again. Cassandra is ours now, and she isn't going anywhere!"

"I liked it when you said I was your son," Marcus said, a kind of catch in his voice.

Kath chuckled, but in her mind she thought, I wish you were my son. I really wish you were!

CHAPTER 10

It was July now. As the days moved deeper into summer Kath became more and more concerned over Marcus's welfare. He seemed depressed, if such a word could be attached to one so young. He came every day, though she could never be sure when he would show up. He still had conversations with her, but sometimes she had to pull anything out of him. If she asked him a question, he would answer with yes or no or not answer at all. It was Cassandra he would hold conversations with. Kath observed them from the window when the two of them were in the yard together, and with the dog at his feet, staring up at him lovingly, Marcus would speak to her, pointing and with gestures. Kath would try to hear what he was saying but could only hear a word here or there. But it was as though the dog understood him and answered him back. Kath simply couldn't understand what she had done to cause him to grow silent toward her.

Every year on the fourth of July there were fireworks in the park. Kath's patio was the perfect observation point. She doubted that Marcus would join her for the event and she sat alone but for Cassandra who lay quietly at her feet. Above her the sky as it grew dark became alive with stars, bright pinpoints of light, and as she had since she was a child, tried to find the brightest ones to wish upon. But on this night her wishes were all for Marcus, that somehow, he would come out of the dark place that he seemed to inhabit. She even said a silent prayer to the universe to send him some help for his current dilemma as she had for herself that winter night which now seemed a long time ago.

And then just as she finished her prayer, Marcus came strolling through the gate, causing Cassandra to jump up and dance around in a circle of bliss. When he and Cassandra were finished with their own personal ritual of greeting Marcus sat down in the chair next to her and as usual was silent. Was she the help she had prayed he might find to help guide him in the right direction, to offer him solace in a time of trouble? But once again she pondered what she could possibly do to help him. Should she go to the authorities and ask them to figure the whole thing out, as far as the abuse and neglect his father seemed to shower on him? But as Marcus had reminded her, things could easily turn out far worse for him if she did that. And so, for the time being at least, she would continue doing what she was already doing, continue to keep an open door to him. They sat there silently for a few moments and then Kath attempted to break the silence. "How did you get away from your father tonight?"

"He went out," Marcus answered, just when Kath was sure he wasn't going to say anything. "He's off getting liquored up somewhere. When he gets home, I'll pretend to be sleeping so he'll leave me alone."

Since she knew Marcus's birthday was in a few days she asked him if there was something in particular, he might want her to give him as a gift. "I don't want anything," he answered. "It's just another day."

"What about a new pair of sneakers?" She asked. "You said you were saving for a new pair of shoes, but I haven't seen you wearing them. What have you been doing with the money you've earned?"

"Oh, my Dad found the place where I was hiding it. He took the most of it. He says I need to start earning my keep!"

Kath shook her head, and was about to say something else but the fireworks had started, lighting the sky with bright streaks of orange, yellow and red. As usual, the burst of color was accompanied by a loud bang and Cassandra's earlier joy at seeing her friend morphed into a mad circle of distress. She rushed to the door and Marcus followed her, the two of them escaping to the safety of the living room. Kath viewed the rest of the fireworks display alone, feeling anxiety and panic at the edge of her own circle of light. But she sat through the rest of the explosions and bursts of color, determined to hold herself and all that surrounded her together.

The next morning, she woke up determined to go out in the car to the shopping center where she could purchase some things for Marcus's birthday. He had left her soon after the fireworks were over the night before and Cassandra had settled down and had even stood still while she hugged him just before he went out the door. "Be careful and take care of yourself," she had said as he was leaving. "I will, Mrs. Longley," he answered. She found herself then and still this morning worrying about what the future held for the boy. He was troubled mentally, she knew that. He was smart though and with a good education he could amount to something. But he wasn't even in a proper school and she doubted his father was paying much attention to his progress.

She had just put Cassandra into the house from her morning ramble in the yard, and was strolling off toward the garage, when someone called to her from the gate. Turning she saw that it was James Gordon from up on the hill. She hurried over to say," Good Morning!"

"I see you were about to go out somewhere," he said, smiling broadly. "I was going to ask if you wanted to take a short walk with me in the park."

"Why I would have loved to," she said, "But could we make it later or better still tomorrow? There's something I've already planned for this morning."

"Why of course we can," he said. "It was just a spur of the moment thing." He paused for a moment staring at her, and she suddenly realized his eyes were blue, just as Fred's had been. With Fred she had often noticed how intense the color could be. Sometimes dull, sometimes bright, just as James Gordon's were this morning.

"Yes, let's make it in the morning," Kath told him, a bit of excitement messing with her feelings. "But first I'll have you in for coffee. Would that be okay?"

"Why that would be splendid," he said. "I can hardly wait."

He left her then but as he crossed the street, he slowed for a moment, looked over his shoulder and gave her a lingering look. She waved as he started up the steps and the path that led to his house.

Driving to the shopping center, Kath wondered if perhaps she should have cancelled her plans to shop for a birthday gift for Marcus. But no, it might have been a bit too forward of her to just abandon her own plans in order to take an unexpected walk with James Gordon in the park. It would be better to wait until tomorrow and it would give her something to look forward to. It had been a bit of a shock to her, and had left her a little ashamed that something had stirred in her when she looked into his eyes at the gate.

Her eyes stung then, and she suddenly thought of Fred. She imagined him sitting next to her in the car. He had left her so unexpectedly there had been no time for a talk as so many couples had at certain times in their lives, all about what they should do if one of them died. All about going on and finding love again and being happy. There had been none of that with Fred. Simply because the two of them had never spoken of such things. It was as though they believed they would just go on together forever.

"Forgive me, Fred," Kath suddenly said, aloud. "I'm just trying to find my way here. You shouldn't have left without saying goodbye."

There was still anger there, but wasn't that part of grieving as Jennifer Winston had told her? Someday she hoped she could release it and be able to take those final smooth steps into life.

She arrived at the Shopping Center then, parked and spent a few moments pulling herself together before going into the Department Store. There were quite a few people at the checkouts as she entered and for a moment a strange, yet familiar feeling of panic rose in her throat, but she grabbed a cart from a lineup near the door, took a deep breath and pushed into the fray. Once into the heart of the store she did not go immediately to the young men's department but investigated a few other places first. In the lady's department she looked at some colorful blouses and a rack of summer dresses. She chose two blouses, a couple of tee shirts, and a cool looking blue flowered dress which was available in her size. Normally she might have taken a long time deciding on a new outfit, but today there were no should I's, is this the right color, or should I simply put everything back? Her choices were instantaneous, and she moved on without thinking. Just beyond the lady's department was a Beauty area with a Hairdresser and a girl who did nails.

It had been a long since she had had anything done to her hair. She knew it was far too long and on warm days she had felt a bit uncomfortable with it hanging down her back. She also knew she would not have the patience to spend the time it would take for a perm. She might be able to tolerate a cut if there would not be a long wait for it.

Enquiring at the front counter, the lady told her she could take her in twenty minutes. The girl who did nails could place her just after that. Although there was a pool of anxiety around her as she thought of sitting in a chair for a long time, not able to move. The thought of running screaming out of the place might have felled her at one time, but today she would face the music. A thought was a thought and she would try dealing with the real situation for a change.

She went to the young men's area then and quickly decided on some tee shirts with the pictures of dogs to start. She chose four of them, though a bit expensive, and put them in the cart. One of the shirts had the likeness of a Westie and she was sure Marcus would like that. She also chose two pair of shorts which looked to her as though they would fit. In the shoe department she chose a particularly expensive pair of walking shoes. She was not sure of sizes, and even though she would probably have to return them, it was important that he at least had them to look at for his birthday. And what did she know of Marcus really? Very little, she realized. What were his likes and dislikes? She had learned a few small things of him. What kind of food he liked, what kind of music, etc. But as for anything about his real life, his future, his hopes and wishes, all that was there were empty blanks.

She returned to the Salon just in time for the friendly girl to lead her to the chair. There was tension at first in her back and arms, but she was able to ignore it and look at some pictures of some shorter cuts that might be like what she had in mind for herself. She chose one with a sinking feeling, and closed her eyes.

"Well what do you think," the girl asked, when she was done with all the pulling and fussing. Kath opened her eyes and hardly recognized the face in the mirror. How long ago had she looked like that, cool and a bit carefree. Fred had always liked her hair long. He liked to run his fingers through it, he had told her, and he often took her brush and run it through it repeatedly. Now that the hair was far shorter than it had been in a long time, tears came to her eyes. Her long hair was gone as Fred was, and he was not coming back. But her hair would grow back. Would she be able to love again?

Later, she had her nails taken care of, nothing fancy, just shaped and polished in a natural tone, and driving home her eyes were drawn to them. The polish was a bit iridescent, and the glittering of the nails in the light made her feel alive.

She stopped at the market and in the Bakery found

a cake that was already iced for a birthday. The girl nodded with a smile when Kath asked if she could add Marcus's name to the cake. She also chose some pastries which she would serve when James Gordon came for coffee in the morning, and later in frozen foods she picked some ice cream to go along with Marcus's cake. And in the card area she chose a birthday card with a Westie face on the front, and a large bag emblazoned with balloons for some of his gifts.

Arriving back home Kath was exhausted. It was the first time in a long time she had gone out and actually done any real shopping, but now that it was done, she realized there had been more enjoyment in it than bad feelings or dread. There was an entirely new path to be walked now and today she had taken one of the first steps.

Marcus's birthday was still a couple of days away but not knowing when he would show up, she arranged his gifts on the coffee table in the living room and placed his cake in the refrigerator. Then she went into a normal routine of getting herself and the house together. After which she lay down in the late afternoon to rest. She was quite excited to see Marcus's reactions to the things she'd gotten him. She hoped he would show up soon so and she intended not only to give him the birthday gifts, but to try a new tact in trying to break through the barrier he seemed to have thrown up lately with his silence and dark mood. She wouldn't question him about anything. She would simply sit and wait and listen. Perhaps then the boy himself would break the silence.

Just before dark he did show up and of course Cassandra rushed to him excitedly and demanded attention. He took her into the yard and they ran together and played ball for nearly an hour. Kath stood at the door and watched. The outdoor lights had attracted bugs and she preferred to stay indoors.

When they did come inside, Marcus seemed a bit winded, but he stood looking at her for a long moment a puzzled look on his face. "What did you do to yourself," he asked. And then his face broke into a smile. "It's the hair," he exclaimed. "You got it cut! You look nice."

"Thank you, Marcus," Kath found herself smiling. "I have a surprise for you." And she led him into the living room where he stood by the coffee table seemingly shocked.

"Are these things for me?" He stood statue like, staring down at the gifts.

"Of course, they're for you. It's your birthday after all."

Marcus sank onto the sofa then and picked up the shoes, opening the box and taking one out to stare at it.

"Try them on," Kath encouraged. And she turned quickly and went into the kitchen where she readied the cake. She found some candles and hurriedly put a few of them on the cake, lit them and carried it into the living room. Marcus had put on the shoes and was sitting staring down at them. He hardly noticed her, or the cake and it wasn't until she said, "Happy Birthday, Marcus," rather loudly, that he looked up and noticed the cake and the candles burning brightly.

His face was happy and sad at the same time. For a moment he sat there as though he didn't know what to say, and then he simply said, "Thank you, Mrs. Longley, you shouldn't have."

"Yes, I should have," she told him. "You deserve this and more. How do the shoes fit? I can take them back and get another size you know."

"No!" He exclaimed! They may be a little big, but I'll grow into them!"

Kath nodded, and stood silently watching.

"You'll grow into them," Marcus spoke softly. "My mother used to say that to me a lot. I miss her."

"I'm sure you do," Kath said. "I'm sure you do."

Marcus seemed to enjoy all the things she had gotten for him. Cassandra hovered at his feet and even had a small dish of ice cream herself when the cake and ice cream were served. After the festivities were over and Marcus had gone, carrying his things and wearing his new shoes, Kath couldn't get the thought of him off her mind. She had carried through with the idea of just remaining silent with Marcus and letting him say what he wanted without her questioning and it had worked up to a point. He had spoken more to Cassandra than he had to her, but that was perfectly okay. The dog seemed to be a kind of healer. Marcus trusted her, and she adored him. He had saved her life after all, and there was an inner bond that had developed between them. Kath understood the whole thing instinctively. She only hoped that someday Marcus would be able to open to her a bit more than he had.

The sky was a bit dark when Kath looked out the window in the morning. Her spirits sank a bit when she realized if it rained her walk with James Gordon would have to be postponed. But luckily the rain held off and the gentleman appeared just after nine, carrying an umbrella.

Kath greeted him at the door warmly. "I was afraid

it might rain," she told him. "I would have been disappointed if it had!"

"Me too," he said. "But I brought my trusted umbrella. Nothing like a walk in the rain to revive you!"

Kath served the coffee and pastries inside since there was a damp feel to the morning air. She found herself tongue tied, but she sat smiling and allowed James Gordon to do most of the talking. She hoped he wouldn't catch her staring. His eyes were a brighter blue than they had been the day before and despite his years he had a youthful look that set him apart. He spoke of his wife and how he spent most of his time keeping up the house indoors and out and doing woodworking in his shop. Cassandra hovered at his feet, staring up at him as though she understood every word he said.

"And what about you," he finally asked, attempting to draw her out. "What have you been doing with your time? Do you miss teaching?"

"Sometimes I think of it and miss it," she said. "But since Fred died it's all I can do to keep myself together. Anxiety and depression, you know. It's been difficult."

"I had the same thing when my wife died," he said, stirring his coffee. "But all of it will pass. Life goes on and we have to find away to move along with it, not allowing it to plow us under."

They finished with the coffee and were ready to go out the door when Kath realized she would have to take Cassandra with them. "I hope you won't mind if she comes along," Kath said ready to attach the leash.

"Of course not," he said reaching down to pat the animal's head. "In fact, I will enjoy it immensely!"

The weather had improved a bit by this time. The clouds were moving away, and streaks of sun were shining down above the park. They were exiting the gate when Marcus suddenly appeared strolling down Park Street. Cassandra noticed him at once and let out a loud bark of greeting.

"Hello Marcus," James Gordon said. "I haven't seen you in a while. What have you been up to?"

"Oh, not much, Mr. Gordon," Marcus said a bit sheepishly.

"We're going for a walk, Marcus," Kath said. "Would you like to come?"

"Yes, but I'll walk ahead with Cassandra," he said and quickly took the dog's leash. The two of them were soon a way ahead of them moving fast.

"So, you know Marcus," Kath said, as they walked. The sun had come out by this time, washing the park in light and dispelling the wisps of fog that had fallen during the night.

"Oh yes, I know him quite well." James said. "His mother came up and helped take care of my wife before she died. She was a big help to us. Marcus was younger then, but he sometimes came along."

"His mother left them you know," Kath told him then. "Last year, I believe."

James Gordon stopped for a moment and stared down at her, a surprised look on his face. "That shocks me a bit," he said. "She doted on the boy. She did often confide in my wife that her husband was quite abusive, and she would like to get away from him, but I never thought she would leave the boy."

"It's affected him very deeply I'm afraid," Kath said. "Especially very recently. He seems depressed and I can't seem to figure it out."

They were silent until they reached the bench at the

top of the hill where they had run into each other a couple of days before. "Shall we sit a spell," James Gordon said. Kath nodded and was about to sit when she realized the bench was covered with a layer of dampness. James Gordon took a handkerchief from his pocket and wiped up the gathered moisture.

"Do you think Marcus has a mental problem," Kath asked after a few moments of silence. "I had a run in with his father right after I first met the boy. He doesn't seem to think I should be bothering with him. He said terribly derogatory things about his son."

James Gordon shook his head and thought for a moment. "He always seemed fairly normal to me," he finally said. "He was very imaginative in those days and his mother said he sometimes made up stories, had imaginary playmates and that sort of thing. He read a lot. How did you become involved with him?"

Kath told him briefly how he had come to her rescue after the snowstorm and about his finding Cassandra behind the garage and saving her life. "I've come to feel responsible for him in an odd sort of way," she said. "But it's quite obviously his father objects to my attention to him. He hinted that he thought it was something sick on my part."

"Yes, he would think that way," James Gordon said. "His wife used to hint he had some deep psychological problems. The father, I'm speaking of now, and not the son. There was a dark cloud hanging over him from his youth when he went to trial for a possible murder."

"Yes, Marcus told me some of that. But after his father hinted that he was a liar and so on, I didn't know what to believe."

They got up from the bench soon after that and

went on with their walk. Nothing more was mentioned of Marcus. Kath caught a couple of glimpses of the boy and the dog ahead of them on the path, but her attention was drawn back each time to James Gordon. She especially liked the way he seemed to pay attention to her, making sure she was comfortable, and that they were not going too fast for her. At rough spots on the path he would steady her with a strong hand on her arm, and when he did so she could feel his warmth and once or twice had an overwhelming desire to put her arm around his back.

They did not take the longer and harder path around the upper part of the Park, but chose the lessor one, that led down through the center and around the baseball diamond, but just as they started down the hill, Kath caught a glimpse of the woods and the railroad in the distance. Her anxiety came back to her in a rush as she thought of the shoe and the shirt that had given her such a start that day.

She suddenly asked him if he had heard about Margorie Winters, the missing girl, feeling instinctively as the words came from her mouth, that it might be the wrong thing to do. And the question did seem to startle James Gordon. An odd look came to his face and he stared down at the path for a moment.

"Odd that you should ask me that," he said finally. "I ran into an old friend of mine just the other day. "He works at the newspaper and I guess he keeps up with these things. We discussed the matter, but it seems everyone believes she ran away from home again."

"Again?"

"Yes, she did run away a couple of years ago when she was fifteen. She was gone for a few days and then returned home. There were rumors she had run off with an older guy, but it was all hushed up."

They arrived back at Kath's gate soon after that and nothing more was mentioned of Margorie Winters. Marcus and Cassandra had already returned and were romping in the yard.

"Will you come in for a few moments," Kath asked, opening the gate.

"No, I'd better head up the hill," James Gordon said. "Nap time now, I'm afraid." He chuckled. "Can we do it again tomorrow, perhaps?"

"I'd like that very much, "Kath told him. "I enjoyed myself."

"I'm glad," he said, still close enough that she could see his eyes flashing. "I'll wait for you here at the gate in the morning."

James Gordon gave her a long look, smiled and walked away, going fast as he went across the street and started up the hill. And then as though he realized she was still standing there at the gate staring at him, he turned, stopped and waved again before continuing.

Kath stood there unable to move for a moment. It was only as James's figure disappeared where the path turned into the hill that she was able to pull away and move toward the house. Marcus and Cassandra were sitting on the grass at the far edge of the yard. Marcus was saying something to the dog and pointing and it was as though they hadn't realized she had returned. Feeling a bit weak after the walk, Kath sank into one of the chairs and sat for a moment thinking and survey-ing her thoughts. A deep feeling seemed to have taken charge of her, if only momentarily. It was the feeling one got when experiencing the joy of a certain kind of human companionship, a feeling she had not had since before Fred died. It was as though a door was opening inside of her and she wanted to walk through the door to see what was happening on the other side. And yet something was blocking the path. And she realized what it was. It was her feelings for Fred. He seemed to stand in front of her with a sad look on his face. How could she ever get past him? She was sitting going over the conversation she had had with James Gordon that morning, every word and tone, when Marcus's voice suddenly interrupted.

"I've got to be going, Mrs. Longley," he said. "My Dad was still in bed this morning and I forgot to hide the things you gave me. If he goes into my room and finds them who knows what he might do with them."

"He wouldn't take them away, surely, or would he?"

"He's liable to do anything. I don't trust him at all."

"Why didn't you wear one of your shirts, and your new shoes?" Kath asked, as the boy was ready to go out the gate. She already noticed earlier he was wearing his usual faded tee shirt and a pair of blue jeans cut offs, and the same worn looking pair of sneakers.

"I'm saving them for good," Marcus said. "My Mom would want me to. Besides just seeing the things would set my Dad off!"

Marcus left her then, but it wasn't until later that evening that Kath realized how true his words had been. She was sitting in the same chair with a glass of iced tea, wishing it was a glass of relaxing wine as in the old days, when someone burst through the gate, startling her and sending fear rushing through her. Twilight had fallen, and darkness was coming fast. The birds and insect sounds were hushed, and she had been sitting in the dark. She should have locked the gate, she realized, and turned on the light. But there was enough light shining from the kitchen windows and the open back door for her to know almost instantaneously that the intruder was Marcus's father. He came charging over to the patio carrying something in his arms and she could hear his heavy breathing.

She got up from the chair at once and rushed into the house where she switched on the lights. When she returned Bart Warner was standing in the center of the lighted patio, a hateful look on his face. He was carrying the gift bag that she had given Marcus the night before. She could tell the man was drunk, by the sour smell of alcohol that permeated the air, and by the way his balance was a bit off as he stood leering at her.

"I see you're buying him clothes now," Bart Warner shouted, his words slurred. "Trying to dress him up, are you? I guess you'll be wanting to show him off next, huh. Well he's a little young for you, isn't he? I don't think your friends will think much of you picking up someone like Marcus. There is a word for that, isn't there? I think it starts with a P..."

Kath's anger was rising by the moment, but it was interspersed with fear. What should she do to rid herself of this hateful man and his sick accusations? Her cell phone was in her purse in the living room. No one would hear her if she called for help.

"Well he doesn't need your clothes," the angry man went on with his hateful rant. "I've brought them back." He threw the bag on the hard cement of the patio. "Why don't you pick someone older, like me?"

Cassandra had come to the inside of the screen door. She had been sleeping in her cage in the living room and had been obviously been awakened by the loud shouting. She was barking now while she jumped at the screen. Luckily the door was closed securely, or she might have burst through and attacked Marcus's father.

"Marcus wants me to tell you he doesn't want anymore to do with you," Bart Warner continued. "In fact, he realizes what a sick woman you are, lusting after a boy his age. And if you don't leave him alone, we're going to turn you into the police. So, let this be a warning."

Kath had stood listening as long as she could. What could she possibly say to defend herself? But now her anger had risen to a dangerous level and as Bart Warner turned, she rushed at him. She wanted to pound him with her fists and how she kept from doing so she had no idea. Instead she simply screamed at him and he turned toward her, obviously startled.

"You sick bastard!" She said, as loud as she could. "I'm the one who should turn you in, and I will, believe me, if you show up here ever again. You have a lot of nerve as it is, bursting in like you have. This is private property and you weren't invited. I think the police will be interested to know how you have beaten Marcus and your wife. They also might like to know that your wife has left you because of your alcoholism and all your sick ways. In fact, I just may go down to the police department tomorrow and report your accusations and all the rest of it."

Kath's words must have sunk in, for Bart Warner turned then quickly without another word and headed toward the gate. A look something like fear had passed over his face.

"I'm not done with you," Mr. Warner. "Remember

that," Kath called after him. "Marcus is welcome any time in my house. I've tried to help him, and I'll continue to do so. But I won't let your sick, defamatory accusations pass..."

He was gone, Cassandra's barks had ceased. Kath picked up the bag the man had thrown down and walked into the house and sank into a chair at the kitchen table, tears in her eyes. Looking in the bag everything she had put there was still in place. The only thing missing was the shoes. But they had been in a separate box. Marcus may have hidden them or put them somewhere that his father hadn't noticed.

What should she do about Marcus? She had to think of something. But it was well past midnight when she finally went upstairs and tried to lay down and sleep and still nothing positive or concrete had come to her. Perhaps in the morning when she walked with James Gordon, she could tell him what had happened and ask for his advice.

CHAPTER 11

It was a troubled and restless night's sleep for Kath. She awoke several times and tossed and turned worrying about what might happen to Marcus. She had been deeply hurt and confused by Bart Warner's drunken behavior the night before. It had left her wracked with all the old feelings of anxiety and panic. But somehow, she had avoided a major attack.

When she did manage to crawl out of bed the next morning around seven, she was still trying to figure out just why he seemed bent on keeping Marcus away from her. Surely, he didn't believe that her interest in Marcus was that sick behavior he had tried to insinuate. The first time he did his best to turn her against the boy, telling her he was mentally challenged, a liar and a thief. But last night he had tried to twist the whole thing around and convince her that Marcus wanted nothing more to do with her, that he too, had suddenly come to believe her interest in him was sick and twisted. But Kath was having none of that. She might be confused by her young friends' current behavior, but she knew it was only a matter of time until he showed up again.

And she was right. She was sitting at the kitchen table making some notes of things she would have to complete before the end of the week. It was Thursday now and on Friday she had dual appointments with her doctor and counselor. The thought of that caused her to and drop her pen and fold her hands together tightly. She was sitting there staring at the window when Cassandra came barking from the living room and almost simultaneously Marcus appeared at the back door.

"My Dad took the things you gave me," he said excitedly when he had come inside and sat down opposite her at the table. His face held a sad, scared look as though she would be angry. "But he didn't get the shoes. I had shoved the box under the bed..."

"I know Marcus," Kath said, feeling a bit low. "He was here again last night. He brought back the bag with your things and threw it down on the patio. Don't worry I have it all inside. Your father said terrible things. He said you never wanted to see me again." Kath was silent for a moment, wiping her eyes with a tissue. Then she lifted her head and looked directly at Marcus. "You know I am only trying to help you. I ... care about you and just want you to have a better life. You do realize that don't you?"

"I know that Mrs. Longley. I never told him that!" Marcus exclaimed, staring down at the table, stroking Cassandra's head with his hands. "He says the same awful things to me. I try not to listen, and I try to avoid him where I can. When he isn't drinking, he has some sane moments. But he's getting worse. I'm never sure what he'll do next. And you should always keep your doors locked, especially after dark."

Marcus went off then with Cassandra. As they were going out the door, he told her his father was still asleep and he wanted to get back home before he woke up. Kath suddenly remembered she was to walk with

James Gordon that morning, and she made herself presentable wearing a pair of shorts and a colorful blouse. She kept her eyes on the gate as she tidied things in the kitchen, but he didn't appear.

It was after nine when Marcus returned with the dog and still James Gordon had not shown himself. Maybe something had happened to him, Kath thought. Maybe he was tired and slept in. And then after Marcus had brought Cassandra back and hurried away again himself, she found herself thinking the most negative thoughts of all. Did she say or do something to offend him? Did she show too much interest when she stared into his eyes, hypnotized by their color? Was it only idle talk when he asked her to walk again, and was he just trying to make a smooth exit? He would probably never walk in the park with her again.

It was after ten when she concluded James Gordon would not walk with her that morning. Wound so tightly with her thoughts Kath decided to take a walk alone, but she would go up the street, away from the park, and perhaps go as far as the market. The morning was clear and bright though it was starting to be a bit warm. Going out the front door she stood for a moment breathing in the sweet summer scents that rose from the stream on the opposite side of the street. A few moments later as she passed the two driveways separated by the wooden fence, she noticed her neighbor Mr. Kline sitting on a chair on his own porch. She threw up her head and looked straight ahead as she walked quickly past. He had totally left her alone since the fence had been built and she liked it that way. Never again would she be bothered by him or his bad behavior.

Kath was nearly at the spot where the hill began

to rise ahead of her when she noticed a group or four or five boys, teenagers obviously, coming toward her. As they drew closer, she could hear their laughter and talk, though she could not make out what they were saying. They had been walking in an irregular pattern, but it seemed that when they noticed her, they walked side by side filling the whole street and blocking her path. The one boy, taller than the rest, with shaved head and arms emblazoned with tattoos, seemed to be the leader. The loudest voice seemed to be coming from him. He spoke like a drill sergeant and the others had turned in his direction. She realized suddenly that they were baiting her, trying to get her to step out of the way to let them pass. But it was a public street after all, and she was suddenly determined to stay in the middle of the sidewalk regardless. If they didn't move, she would simply plow into them. She was only a few inches away, could nearly hear them breathing, when suddenly they separated to let her pass. She said nothing as she walked looking straight ahead but hearing laughter and obviously nasty comments behind her, she turned and glared back at them. They were laughing and jostling and pointing but Kath stood there defiantly. Once they were a bit further along, they turned away and she continued up the hill, feeling a bit triumphant.

It suddenly occurred to her that these were probably the boys who had built the camp in the woods. Marcus had said they got there from the railroad and that there was a path leading up to the embankment just beyond the bridge. Since they passed her house to get there, was it possible they had stolen the furniture off her porch?

She let the thoughts of the boys go then as she was approaching Geraldine Harvey's house. Peering ahead with the sun in her eyes she saw that the porch was empty. She had hoped that her nemesis might have been sitting there this morning, and she could have stopped and attempted once again to confront her over her unfair attacks.

Kath walked slower as she approached the house. She stopped at the foot of the stairs and thought of how easy it would be to climb them and knock on the door. But peering up she saw that the door had been left slightly ajar. The morning sounds of the town ahead had grown louder as she walked. There were horns blowing and brakes screeching and off in the distance the sounds of children laughing. But closer at hand if she listened there was the sound of someone calling for help. The words were distinct, "Help me, Help me!"

The voice was quite close in fact, and with a twist of her head she realized that it was coming from inside the house. At first, she had no idea what she should do, but when the call for help came again, louder and sounding far more desperate, Kath quickly mounted the stairs. Arriving at the door she gingerly grabbed the knob and opened it completely.

"Hello," she called, trying to quell the waver in her voice. "Are you hurt? Can I help you?"

"Yes, I need... help." The voice from inside sounded raspy now. "I fell...I fainted."

The voice impediment, although clearly under-standable, was that of Geraldine Harvey. Kath quickly entered the room. The space was sparsely furnished, though quite neat and clean. A sofa and a chair and a couple of tables were the only furniture, but magazines and a few books were neatly stacked, and a faded print of horses hung above one of the tables.

The voice came from a doorway at the end of the room. "Back here," the voice called. "In the hallway!"

Kath rushed to the door and through it. Geraldine Harvey lay sprawled on the floor her one leg seeming to lay at an odd angle.

It's Mrs. Longley from down the street," Kath said as she knelt to take the ladies hand. "Do you know who I am?"

She half expected Geraldine Harvey to lash out at her, but instead she said, "Yes, you're Professor Lonely from the college." The impediment in her voice caused her to drop letters, and it was growing weaker now and she was obviously in pain.

Knowing from the position the lady was laying in she should not be moved, quickly reached into her purse, her hands shaking, and pulled out her cell phone.

"I'm calling an ambulance," Mrs. Harvey. "I think you may have broken something. What is your house number?"

"It's 823, please tell them to hurry. Its bad, the pain is awful bad."

Kath dialed 911 quickly and gave the dispatcher the details. Then she kneeled and spoke soothingly to Geraldine Harvey, attempting to help her remain calm. As she did so she noticed close-up how thin the lady had become. Her flowered summer house dress seemed to hang on her frame.

"How long have you been lying here, Mrs. Harvey?" Kath asked. "I was walking to the market when I heard you call out."

"It seems like hours," the lady said. "I was up... before dawn."

"Try to hold on now, the ambulance will be here soon."

And it was only a few minutes later when she heard the loud sound of the siren and suddenly a sharp knock on the door. Two burley looking men carrying a stretcher and a medical bag pushed into the room without her even having to open it, and she led them to the hallway where Geraldine Harvey lay.

"Are you a relative," one of the men asked, while the other one took vitals signs and readied Mrs. Harvey for the stretcher.

"No, just a neighbor passing by," Kath told him. "I heard her calling for help. All I know is her name, Geraldine Harvey."

"Could you check for a purse, perhaps," the man asked. "They'll need some info at the hospital!"

"I don't know if I should do that," Kath hesitated.

"Just look around, please," he said firmly. This is an emergency."

Kath quickly went back into the living room and found a brown leather bag sitting open on the sofa. She gingerly closed it and carried it back to the hallway where the men had already placed Geraldine Harvey onto the stretcher. She stood back while the men went into action and followed as they carried Mrs. Harvey from the house into the back of the ambulance. "Is there someone I should call," She asked, handing over the purse she had found just before they were ready to close the door. But there was no answer from the prone figure who the two attendants had covered with blankets. Kath wondered if perhaps Mrs. Harvey had slipped into unconsciousness. She stepped up unto the sidewalk and stood watching as the men closed the door, and then jumped inside. The ambulance rushed off, siren wailing, and Kath stood there for a moment not knowing which direction she would go in.

She finally made the decision to walk back toward home. After her morning experience she was left feeling anxiety creep suddenly along her back. A visit to the market might be a little more than she could take right now on top of everything else. It was odd, she thought, walking back along Bridge Street, sunlight flickering through the leaves of the maples that grew along the street, that she had waited for a long time for the opportunity to confront Geraldine Harvey for her gossip and all the unkind things she had been saying about her, and then to have met her again in such an unbelievable and unexpected way. Her anger seemed to have failed her but then she realized she was very glad that it had. She was never a person who had allowed anger, although it was present, to control her. Sometimes life had a way of turning things around, causing one to face something they had avoided or even to face truth because it was staring them in the face. Perhaps she hadn't been angry at Geraldine Harvey at all, but only angry at herself because she hadn't had enough empathy to understand.

Later that afternoon, Kath was sitting with Cassandra on the sofa in the cool living room brushing the dog's fur. Marcus had bathed her a couple of times in the past weeks, but Kath realized she would soon have to have a professional grooming. She was a real mess. She could easily clip the hair away from the dog's eyes, but it would be a lot cooler if she had a full treatment. Another task to be completed soon. She couldn't stop thinking of Geraldine Harvey. Did she have a family somewhere who should be notified, children perhaps, or even a close friend who would be wondering what had happened to her? Kath hated hospitals and the thought of visiting someone there was a bit more than she was willing to manage. And after all, was it something she should even feel responsible for? But as a human being she realized she should at least try to find out how the woman was doing. Was she dead or alive, would they keep her in the hospital or send her home? Whether she liked it or not, when she was out the next day at the medical building, she would have to drive the extra mile to the hospital to check in on Mrs. Harvey.

When Kath was about to lie down later for a nap, her mind having calmed a bit from her morning adventures, the house phone rang. She picked it up on the kitchen extension and was surprised to hear James Gordon's voice. "Kath, I'm sorry about this morning," he said. "I had unexpected visitors last evening. An old friend of mine from New England stopped by. We were in the Navy together. They spent the night…"

"You don't have to explain," Kath interrupted. "I assumed something had come up." She kept her voice as calm as possible hoping that he didn't detect her earlier disappointment.

"I'm glad you understand!" She at least could detect his obvious sincerity. "Why don't we try again in the morning? I was really looking forward to seeing you again and continue getting reacquainted…"

"I would love that," she said. "Only if you stop in first for coffee before we take to the path."

"Of course," he said, with a slight chuckle, "of course!"

Later as she was lying on the bed trying to rest, she couldn't stop thinking of James Gordon. What was wrong with her that she was remembering every word he had said, even down to the tone of his voice. And at the same time, she was visualizing his expressive blue eyes and his hand on her arm at certain rough places on the trail. When she finally did drift into a light sleep, she dreamed about walking along a path with a gentleman. But the face changed from place to place. One time it was Fred and then it was James Gordon, and when he leaned down and kissed her, she realized it was not her husband.

She had not had much sleep after that. In fact, she had awakened and then lay there trying to analyze her own feelings. There was a thin line between excitement and guilt. If Fred were still alive, she could understand the guilt. But he wasn't, and James Gordon was, and he was close at hand. In the morning she would walk with him again and the thought of him being there next to her caused her breath to catch in her throat.

Kath had the shock of her life when she woke from her nap in the afternoon. She had heard a rather loud dog bark and when she opened her eyes it sounded again and looking down, she saw Cassandra standing at the edge of the bed staring up at her. The dog had somehow climbed the stairs for the first time obviously to be near her. A few times before she had walked with her to the foot of the stairs, but had always turned and gone back to the safety of her cage.

Finding the dog at her feet, Kath crawled from the bed and reached down and patted the animal. It gave her a good feeling to know that the dog wanted to be near her. Was this something she would have to expect from now on? She didn't have the heart to lock the animal into her cage. And how would she get back downstairs again? Kath wondered if she had the strength to carry her back down. But she needn't have worried. Cassandra followed her to the stairs and then down them again doing one step at a time! Kath reached the bottom of the stairs and looked back to see the dog put all four feet on one step before proceeding to the next. She showed no fear or hesitation but once down the stairs followed Kath into the kitchen and went to the door wanting to be let out.

Kath shook her head and once she had poured a glass of iced tea for herself, she went out to the patio and sank into one of the chairs, her attention drawn to Cassandra who was moving slowly around the perimeter of the yard as though she were on patrol.

Life is full of small miracles, she thought as she sat there sipping her tea. It was one of those pure, warm summer afternoons when the sun had sunk low on the horizon and the sounds of the day were hushed. Even the birds seemed to be finishing their days chores and were off in the trees asleep. It had been a miracle that the dog had survived at all, a miracle that Cassandra had learned as quickly as she did that, she and Marcus had rescued her from whatever awful life she had lived before and were simply trying to help her? And now this new unexpected miracle that the dog had followed her up the stairs to her bedroom. Had it simply been because she wanted to be near her, to protect her? A small miracle indeed but one that she was grateful for. And what of the major miracle of Marcus's appearing at her front door that morning after the storm? She would always think it had been a miracle indeed but there was also a curse at the edge of it, his awful father and the uncertainty of where the boy's life was going.

Early the next morning she was still thinking of miracles. Did life simply move on from day to day in a kind of random pattern, or was there a force behind it, a god-like force if you will, one that led each person on a life long journey, like riding a driverless car that saw and knew everything and all we had to do was simply go along for the ride? And as she prepared the table and sat out mugs and a tray of fruit and pastries she thought of James Gordon. Was he a miracle too? But how could he be a miracle when he had lived next door on the hill for years? And when did the moment occur when a simple bit of reality become a miracle? Had it been when she first heard his voice again after years of silence, or when she first noticed the life that pulsated deep in his eyes, causing her to realize she was still alive too?

This was the first time in a long time that she had been able to let her mind wonder from one philosophical thought to another. It had been that way when she was still at work at the college, when one of the students or a book or author they had been following had led her down a path to a new land. And then her mind had been taken over by her fear and anxiety and the driverless car had gone into the ditch waiting for rescue and repair.

She was still thinking crazy thoughts of such things when a knock came to the back door. Was it James Gordon? It wasn't quite seven thirty, and she wasn't ready. No, it was Marcus. He greeted her with a smile and Cassandra with hugs and kisses.

"She came up the stairs to my bedroom yesterday, in the afternoon," Kath told him. It was a bit of a shock, but I was happy to see her. Last night she went right into her cage."

"She's smarter than we realize," Marcus said. "She knows what I'm thinking sometimes. It's a bit of a miracle don't you think?"

Kath didn't answer but watched as Marcus put her leash around her neck and waved as they went out the door for a walk.

I'd better put my miracles away for a while, Kath thought. Otherwise I might just begin to fly.

James Gordon appeared at the door a few moments later, wearing a white shirt and a light pair of shorts. He had on a pair of sun glasses which he removed once they were sitting opposite each other at the table. "I think it may be warmer than usual today," he said. "Much as I enjoy our conversations, perhaps we should get started before long. That path can be a real trial in the heat."

"Yes, it can be difficult," Kath said, especially that last one on the upper trail?"

James Gordon chuckled. "Yes, you are right, but I'll show you the best way to deal with that."

And how would that be," Kath asked, fussing with his coffee and pulling the pastries close to where he was sitting, all the while noticing small details of the man, how his graying hair seemed to curl over his ears and the widening grin on his lips.

"We'll just walk in the opposite direction," he said. "It's just the one steep hill and mostly going down from there. You'll see."

James Gordon led her back along the identical route

she and Marcus had taken that day they had found the shirt and the shoe. It was one of those perfect summer mornings, the kind you dream about in winter sleep, where the temperature is cool enough, and the sun is low enough in the sky where you don't have the squint and only the horizon is covered with a low hazy mist. Kath had always loved the look of the park on mornings like this, and sometimes gazing out at it from her kitchen window, she had longed to be there. Now she was here, and she felt quite a bit safer knowing that this gentleman was by her side.

James Gordon did most of the talking as they walked. He was a keen observer of nature, she noticed, and pointed out various plants and small animals as they walked. But one thing that particularly pleased her was that he kept his eye on her, pointed out rough places on the path and held on to her arm when he thought she might need his support.

As they drew closer to the fence and the woods a bit of fear rose in her. There didn't seem to be a reason for fear on a morning like this, but it was there at the back of her thinking. Coming back to the place from the opposite direction was like having to face her fear. A book on anxiety she had read had said that sometimes we have the do the things we fear, go back to places that have terrified us, and simply get out of the house if we have agoraphobia, even if it causes an attack. We must stand and face and not run away from our demons.

"Are you alright," James said, seeming to notice the taut look that had suddenly crossed Kath's face. She was staring at the woods as they walked. This morning with the sun low in the sky it was a dark jungle of a place, filled with weeds and vines and dark trees that seemed to hang over the fence. From place to place a tree had grown through the fence only to be snipped off by the park workers.

"I'm okay," she said, "I don't like the woods. I guess I'm a little afraid of the unknown."

"There's nothing to be afraid of. It's just simply a nature preserve there," James Gordon said, soothingly. "The railroad owns the land and they keep it like that to protect the wild things."

By this time, they had reached the bench at the bottom of the steep hill where she had met Marcus and Cassandra that day when she had walked the path part of the way alone.

"Let's sit here a spell," James said, taking her arm as she sank down to the bench. Kath was breathing a bit deeply, and he seemed concerned.

"Are you're sure you're doing okay," he went on. "Perhaps we should have taken the easier route."

"Oh no I'm fine," Kath told him. "I will just have to get used to walking here. I'm just a bit winded."

They were silent for a few moments. James Gordon's observant eyes were everywhere. Kath couldn't tear her own eyes away from the woods where she imagined she saw a dark shape move among the bushes and vines. "Marcus says some boys may have a camp of some sort over there," she said.

"I suppose they may," he told her. "You know how boys are, they always seem to want to go where they aren't wanted. I was one of them long ago." He chuckled then. "I know where you're coming from Kath," he said then seriously. "When you've been through all you've been through fear can sometimes take control of us if we let it. I was that way after my wife's death. It wasn't easy getting back to myself, but I finally made it. You will, too."

Hearing James Gordon's kind words, and feeling his understanding gave Kath a sudden rush. A few moments later he helped her up from the bench and they went forward to conquer the hill. Arriving there, and looking up, the whole thing seemed quite formidable. But James Gordon took her arm and they went up a few steps.

"The secret is to go a short distance and then to rest and not look back, okay?"

Kath nodded, and they walked up a few more. And she found the whole things was easy just as he had told her. Near the top she did stumble a bit and James Gordon's arm quickly surrounded her. He held her steady for a moment and she looked up at him and he was looking down at her with an odd look in his eyes. They were wide and there was a bit of moisture on his upper lip. She recognized the look. There was a bit of longing and passion there and whatever James Gordon was feeling she was feeling it as well. He looked away suddenly as though he did not want her to know he was human too.

They reached the top of the hill and James Gordon went back to be his usual self. They were starting down the long incline toward the bottom when Marcus and Cassandra suddenly appeared at a curve in the path. Cassandra rushed forward, obviously happy to see her, but something was wrong with Marcus. His face was white and taut, and he looked a bit frightened.

"Oh Mrs. Longley," he said. "I'm glad I've run into you. I'm not feeling well. Can you take Cassandra with you and I'll just go straight back home?"

"What is it Marcus, Kath asked. "You look ill. Maybe you should just go back with us in case you get to feeling worse."

"No, I'll be okay." He said, his voice a bit ragged. "I just need to be alone now."

He gave Kath Cassandra's leash and without even saying goodbye to Cassandra, he went off down the hill at a hurried pace, leaving the dog confused and staring up at her.

"I wonder what that was all about," Kath said, looking after him.

"Something must have happened," James Gordon said. "It must have been something unpleasant to have him behaving like that."

CHAPTER 12

They walked the rest of the path in silence, all the while Kath was thinking of Marcus. Beside her James Gordon continued to be attentive, and at one point he seemed to know where her thoughts were, for he stopped and looked down at her. "I'm sure Marcus will be okay," he said. "You mustn't get yourself so upset by any behavior of his. It hasn't been an easy life for him and now that his mother's gone, I'm sure it can be a challenge."

"I know it shouldn't bother me," Kath said. They were close to home by this time and Cassandra was pulling on her leash as though she was expecting Marcus to be waiting when they arrived back. "But I have just been trying to help him. It doesn't seem right that he should be dealing with so much..."

"You have to put yourself first now," James said when they had arrived back at the gate. "If you don't heal yourself first how can you help the boy?"

Kath didn't answer, but stood looking up at him trying to smile. James Gordon hesitated as though he didn't want to leave her and go up the hill. Finally, he said, "Lets do this again soon, okay?" Then after a kind of awkward pause he added, "Better still, would you go out to dinner with me sometime, Kath?" The words seemed to slip from his lips and after they were said, he looked at the ground as though he was afraid he had gone a bit too far.

"Of course, I would," Kath spoke quickly. "It would be my pleasure!"

"Great!" James said, his face brightening. "We'll set a date soon, I promise!"

He turned and crossed the street then without looking back. Kath stood watching until he had climbed the stairs and disappeared at the turning of the path. She went inside then, Cassandra, free of her lease, went through the house as though expecting Marcus to be there waiting.

"Marcus will be back," Kath said to the dog. "Very soon. You'll see."

There was just too much to be thought about, to be worried over, she realized as she tried getting back into the routine of her day. So many things she needed to remember to talk with Dr. Barker and Jennifer Winston about when she had her appointments with them that afternoon.

But by the time she had worked her way through ring after ring of anxiety, when she had finally arrived at Dr. Barker's office at precisely 130, she had forgotten everything she had wanted to discuss with him. There was no need to worry however since the doctor did most of the talking. And he seemed pleased with her progress. "You've come a long way," Kath," he told her, a hopeful look on his face. "You seem like you've gotten better control of your situation."

"I have my bad days," she told him. "But better than bad, I think."

"And are you still staying away from the alcohol?"

"I haven't had a drink in a long time," she told him.

"There has been a bit of a craving, but I have been able to control that."

"The medication seems to be doing its work," Dr. Barker said. "And while I don't want you to stop taking it, I do think perhaps we should start weaning you back a bit. What do you think?"

"I agree," Kath said. "I don't want to become an addict. But what if its too much and I go back..."

"You're not going to go backwards," Kath. "If you notice a major change in the way you're feeling, call me at once. We can always adjust and readjust. I have the greatest confidence that you will continue to move forward."

Kath was feeling a bit more optimistic when she arrived in Jennifer Winston's office a short time later. It was always good to know that the Doctor would be there for her and she could call him if she got into a bad situation. And now there were so many things she wanted to discuss with the counselor. And where would she start? There was layer after layer of concerns and where would she find the thread to begin?

But Jennifer Winston always made it so easy to begin. It was obviously the way she made her feel, calm, confidant. It was the sincere look the therapist always had on her face, and the way her voice sounded, like a breath of fresh air. This afternoon Mrs. Winston seemed even friendlier, even kinder if such a thing was possible. Or was it just the fact that she was feeling a kind of high due to James Gordon's interest in her? No matter, it was Mrs. Winston's questioning of her anger level that opened the door for her to discuss her life and concerns, and then bring up once again her meeting James Gordon after such a long time.

"But you seem a bit hesitant and unsure of your-self," Mrs. Winston said when Kath paused for a moment, seeming to have lost her train of thought. "What are you really feeling?"

"I can't get past the idea that Fred is standing in the way," Kath finally blurted. "I feel a bit guilty."

"Are you still angry at him because he died and left you?"

"Yes, those feelings are still there. But I'm confused. I find myself responding to James Gordon's obvious interest in me, but I feel if I go any further, I'm being unfaithful to Fred."

"It's very normal that you are feeling that way." Mrs. Winston told her. "You loved your husband very much. It is your memory that is blocking your path. Fred is not coming back ever again. That's the fact. But you are still dealing with the loss. Anger is a natural emotion on our way through grief. Have you tried, as I suggested, to speak to him?"

"I've tried, but I find it difficult."

"Write him a letter, go to his grave and speak to him as though he is really there. Don't give up. You'll work your way through this eventually. I know you will."

Before leaving the therapist's office, Kath recounted her experience of trying to confront Geraldine Harvey and then finding the lady calling out for help and going to her aid.

"It's strange, isn't it," Mrs. Winston said with a smile, as Kath was ready to leave, "The way life seems to work things out for us as we go along. If we just try to do the right thing and keep plugging away, fate seems to come to our aid, doesn't it?"

Driving away from the medical complex Kath found

her tensions begin to mount. It wasn't the idea of visiting Geraldine Harvey, it was the thought of entering the hospital itself that had thrown the switch. The place had such bad memories for her, the sickness, the reality of age and of death. Somehow her fear of the unknown never seemed to leave her. And arriving at the place a few moments later she found nothing had changed. A dark cloud seemed to hang over the building despite the brightness of the day. She parked at the back of the lot, somehow it was easier to wind herself through the confusion of the cars and sad looking people hurrying about, than it was to get up too close where the reality of the place might try to adhere itself.

With the help of a stern looking woman at the front desk she found out where Geraldine's Harvey room was located, near the end of a hall on the third floor. Before stepping into the elevator, she went into a gift shop nearby. She found a small bouquet of miniature pink roses which she felt would be appropriate to give to the lady who she barely knew. Her hands shook as she paid for it at the register.

Room 381 was located just a short distance from the elevator. Other than two bored looking nurses at a desk the floor seemed to be empty. The antiseptic smell of the place was almost more than Kath could handle and she had to swallow hard to keep from coughing. Geraldine Harvey was alone in a room with two beds. She appeared to be asleep in the bed near the window.

Grasping hard at her courage, Kath approached the bed. The lady's eyes were closed, and she seemed to be breathing normally.

"Hello Mrs. Harvey," Kath said, a bit hesitantly, "are you awake?"

There was no movement from the bed, so Kath spoke again, a bit louder. "Mrs. Harvey, are you awake?"

The woman's eyes opened suddenly, appearing quite large in the pale looking face, with the gray hair spread out around her head on the white pillow. At first it seemed she wasn't quite aware of where she was and then she looked up and stared directly into Kath's eyes.

"How are you feeling Mrs. Harvey," Kath asked, holding the bouquet closer, hoping the lady could catch a whiff of the roses.

"I brought you some flowers, Mrs. Harvey. Do you remember me?"

"Yes," the woman spoke after a long moment, her voice raspy. She cleared her throat. "You're Mrs. Lonely from down at the college. You found me."

She reached up with a steady hand and took the bouquet from Kath's hands. She stared at the roses for a moment and then held them close to her face. "They smell so nice. No one ever brought me flowers before. Thanks."

She handed the flowers back to Kath and found the switch that raised the bed. When she had maneuvered it to a better position, she stopped it and sat staring at Kath for a moment, her face taut.

"You don't seem to be the person I thought you was," she said. "I thought you was uppity, stuck up, you know..."

"I tried to get to know you, Mrs. Harvey. I tried."

"Yes, but I didn't know anybody like you. You seemed to know everything." Mrs. Harvey looked away and wiped her lips with the back of her hand.

"You see I came from up in the valley. We lived on the farm. I had to quit school to help with the cows and all the chores. We were poor. I've been poor all my life. I guess I was jealous of you..."

"It doesn't matter, Mrs. Harvey. I was just lucky," Kath said. "You could have been something too, if you had had a chance..."

"If I could have been, I would have been," Geraldine Harvey spoke firmly. "No need to think of what might have been."

Kath sat the bouquet on the bedside stand. "Are you feeling better," she asked then. "Is your hip going to be okay?"

"They didn't tell me much," Geraldine Harvey told her. "They just said it wasn't broke, just badly bruised. And something about my blood I didn't understand."

"I'll come back again to see you," Kath finally said after a few more moments of exchanging pleasantries.

"They may send me home..."

"Then I'll come to visit you there," Kath told her. "I'll keep in touch." She reached down and covered Geraldine Harvey's cold hands with her own, hoping the woman could feel the warmth she hoped was there. She said goodbye then and left the room.

Just as she was about to head to the elevator, she encountered a nurse hurrying in her direction.

"I'm sorry to bother you," Kath said, "But could I speak to you for a moment?" The nurse stopped and nodded, staring off down the hall toward somewhere she needed to be in a hurry.

"I'm enquiring about Mrs. Harvey in room 381. Is she going to be all right?"

"I didn't think she had any family."

"I'm not family. I live up the street. I found her."

The nurse looked around her hesitantly. Seeing no

one nearby she turned back to Kath. "It's against the rules to give out information, but in this case, I don't see how it can matter. "The lady has cancer. Her prognosis is not good. We're going to send her home in a day or two, with a nurse and hospice. Her hip is only bruised, but she hasn't much time..."

The news shocked Kath to the core. The drive back home was more difficult than she had expected. By the time she had arrived home she was in the throes of an attack of panic. She allowed Cassandra to have a run in the yard, and then went into the living room and sank into the sofa. By this time, it seemed to her, the attacks had become fewer and further between. But they still had a sting and a bite, and it was hard not to feel fear as the waves of anxiety washed over her.

She sat there for what seemed a long time going over the day in her mind. Perhaps she had done too much, and there was still a lot to be worried about. Her thoughts went from Mrs. Harvey, to James Gordon and then back again to Marcus. What had caused his strange behavior in the park that morning? Had he become ill or had some twist of fate, an encounter perhaps, caused him to run off in a hurry as though he were afraid? Eventually Kath was able to calm herself enough to begin the relaxation technique that Jennifer Winston had given her on a previous visit. And after slowly attempting to relax each part of her body, and breathing in a slow and methodical manner, she fell into a peaceful sleep.

It wasn't until the following evening, just as it began to get dark that she saw Marcus again. She was sitting on the patio with a glass of tea, Cassandra lying calmly at her feet, when the dog jumped up, barking loudly and went running toward the gate, tail wagging. It was Marcus, and after he had slipped inside the yard and had the usual meet and greet with Cassandra, he came and sank quietly into the chair opposite her.

"I was worried about you," Kath said. "Are you okay? Why did you run away like that?

Marcus was silent for a long moment and Kath stared in his direction, though the evening darkness made it hard for her to see his face or gauge his reaction.

"I didn't feel well," he said then. "I've been having nightmares. As Cassandra and I were walking I saw some boys in the distance near the baseball field. It looked like those boys who have the camp in the woods and it made me remember one of my dreams."

"What kind of dream did you have?" Kath asked, trying to keep her voice calm. Though inside she was not calm at all.

"It was about those boys, something I saw them doing, though it didn't seem like a dream at all. It seemed real."

"Do you want to tell me about it?"

"I will sometime," he said after another long pause. "I'll tell you about it..."

Kath didn't question him again. It seemed the best thing to just remain silent. Marcus would have to come to her if he needed someone to talk to.

Marcus left her soon after that, as quickly as he had come. At bedtime, Cassandra followed her up the stairs again, and later stood at the side of the bed and whined and wouldn't stop until Kath had got up and lifted her unto the bed beside her. The dog instinctively burrowed into the covers next to her and lay down with a sigh. Cassandra seemed a little scared. Was she afraid for herself or was she picking up the fact that Kath was a little afraid also and perhaps needed protection and companionship?

The next day, Sunday, the weather changed. The sunlight and warmth of the past few days were replaced by a darkening sky and swirling clouds to the west. Rain was forecast, though perhaps it wouldn't arrive until the next day, and there was a distinct chill in the air. Kath had decided earlier that this might the time when she could drive out to the cemetery and visit Fred's grave. Perhaps it would be better to wait until a time when the weather was brighter and more favorable. But no, she would go despite the clouds and the threat of rain. She would take an umbrella, and what would it matter if she got a little damp? She dressed warmly in slacks and a sweater and it was just after noon when she started out the door.

She was just about to lock it when Marcus came strolling across the yard. He stopped at the edge of the patio.

"Are you going out, Mrs. Longley," he asked. "I was going to take Cassandra for a walk."

"I'm going out to the cemetery to visit my husband's grave," she told him. "But you can come, too, if you'd like. We can take Cassandra and you can walk with her out there. What do you say?"

Marcus hesitated, and then he nodded his head and said, "Okay, I'll come along."

It was the first time Cassandra had ever ridden in the car, but she behaved rather well. She sat on the seat between the two of them and looked from side to side at the passing scenery. It was a short four mile drive out to the Memorial Gardens. Kath made one quick stop at the Market and purchased a fresh flower bouquet to place on the grave. She felt a bit guilty that she had not taken flowers to Fred's grave before this, but she hadn't been ready. Today she felt she was as ready as she would ever be.

Arriving at the Memorial Gardens there were a few cars in the lot at the bottom of the hill, but Kath drove up a narrow road at the edge of the graveyard to where there was a pull off place. She could park there and walk the few yards to the grave.

"You can take Cassandra down the hill for a walk," Kath said to Marcus after she'd parked, and they got out of the car. "Just stay on the roadway. I don't think dogs are allowed here. I'll be a little while."

Marcus nodded, attached Cassandra's leash and they were off. Kath took the flowers and walked slowly to the top row and then veered off to the third double set of graves. The gray granite stone was topped by raised letters, Longley. And underneath to the one side was Fred's name chiseled into the stone, along with the dates which she wanted to forget.

Kath turned her eyes away and gazed down hill to where the land rolled away in a series of farms and fields. Off to the south a gray mist was slowly drifting in. To her right she could see the outskirts of Bridgetown on the horizon, the trees and jagged outlines of buildings vivid in the stark afternoon light. In the distance and moving further down the hill on the road that led along the lines of graves, she could see Marcus and Cassandra moving slowly away from her.

She had a sudden desire to be there with them. They were they only living things she could make out. All around where she stood there was silence and the remnants of death. She had to reach deeply into her mind and memory to find Fred. He most certainly was not here in the reality of this place. She never could understand why so many people found solace here among the stones and the vague thoughts of what lay underground.

Kath closed her eyes hard and then wiped away a tear that had escaped from the corner of one eye. When she opened them again the atmosphere seemed to have changed. She could see bits of color again, most notably in the flowers she held in a shaking hand. She lay them down in front of Fred's name on the stone. Then she raised her eyes to the sky where the clouds were swirling. She imagined Fred was up there somewhere and that she could see his face smiling at her through a window in the clouds.

She was finally able to speak, and though her voice wavered she tried keeping it at a normal tone. "Oh, dear Fred," she said, "I wish I could find you here somewhere in the flesh and take you home again. But I realize more than ever that you're not here. You're out there in space somewhere or off in another dimension, in a form and shape I could never understand. All I have of you is a memory. And I realize, coming here today, that it is silly of me to be angry at a memory. Because in my mind you are smiling at me, still loving me as you always have. You were the best husband I could ever have found. It was fate and not your fault that took you away from me."

She paused for a moment and saw through her tears that Marcus and Cassandra had turned and were slowly making their way back up the hill. "Don't be angry at me Fred for trying to make my way back into life again. Down there are the things that matter. They have my heart. And I'm becoming acquainted with our neighbor again, James Gordon, remember him? He reminds me of you. He has your eyes, and he's very kind, just as you were. I know you'll approve of my need for being human. Just know when I leave here today you are going with me. Because I finally know where you are. You're in my mind and heart just as I remember you. And if I can breathe, I'll hold you there and keep you safe wherever I am."

It started to rain just as she was heading back toward the car. It was suddenly coming down in a rush and there was a rumble of thunder in the distance. Below her Marcus and Cassandra were running toward her, obviously wanting to stay dry. Kath had left the umbrella on the back seat of the car, but she continued walking at a normal pace. The rain on her face, was refreshing, healing. The trip to the cemetery had finally convinced her she was still alive and soon would be completely well again.

CHAPTER 13

The rain that started that afternoon in the cemetery, continued into the next several days. It would either be raining when Kath awoke in the morning or it would begin in the afternoon, with thunder and lightning and huge downpours. By mid-August she was beginning to believe a monsoon was upon them and that the whole of Bridgetown would be inundated by a flood of Noah's proportions.

But besides a few overflows of Anderson's Creek in the lower sections of town, nothing of biblical proportions occurred. The land had been dry and much in need of rain and seemed to soak up with relish this manna from the clouds. Kath herself had never disliked rainy days or been anxious over flooding or disaster. For as long as she had lived in Bridgetown, Anderson's Creek had only had brief periods where it rose up to where the surface could be seen from her window.

The house was shipshape, Fred had seen to that. The roof was new and the tree that had been felled by the wind during the winter storm had done no real damage and had left only a few scratches on the siding once the city maintenance department had sawed it up and hauled it away. Kath felt safe in her cocoon even during the worst of the stormy weather.

Cassandra on the other hand would escape to her

cage when thunder crashed outside. She would go to the door and want out only when the urge to relieve herself was strongest, and then would bark to be back in after only a few moments in the yard. Marcus still came at intervals but for the most part the two of them would romp in the living room. Marcus would throw the ball and the dog would half-heartedly retrieve it.

One afternoon Kath sat him down and explained to Marcus that this might be the best time to call Dr. Riley, so they could have Cassandra spayed. It would be a simple surgery. If they left her as she was there would always be the risk of infection later and that could be life threatening.

Marcus hugged the dog and seemed frightened when she brought it up, but once Dr. Riley dropped by the following day and explained the whole thing to him, he seemed more relaxed. The doctor didn't perform surgeries in his van but took the animals to a clinic where he had access. He took Cassandra away early one morning, much to Kath's chagrin, and returned her later that afternoon. She was awake and seemed none the worse for wear.

"Just call me if she seems ill or if the wound seems swollen or irritated. I'll come right away," he told her.

But Cassandra went on with life as she always had and, in a day or two, seemed as though nothing at all had happened. Marcus seemed quite happy that the dog was recovering well, but Kath noticed that the boy himself seemed to be sinking into a kind of depressed state that never quite seemed to leave him. When she questioned him about what might be wrong, he would make excuses and change the subject.

One morning when there was a lull in the rain, James Gordon showed up at the back door with his umbrella and they went for a short walk in the park. At the bench on top of the hill he wiped the damp surface with a handkerchief so that Kath could sit down. They sat there silently for a moment or two while Kath surveyed the park before them, bathed in mists and wisps of fog. The sky was dull and dark, and the air was pure though a bit chill. Kath glanced at James Gordon as they sat there. He too was gazing out over the landscape and seemed to be deep in thought. Kath wondered if he was just older or a bit of a fluke but how many men still carried handkerchiefs in a back pocket to wipe a damp bench so that a proper lady could sit down?

He finally turned to her with a sheepish grin on his face. "There's a little Chinese restaurant down at the end of Bridge Street and I was wondering if you'd like to go there with me tomorrow night. They have a lovely buffet and it's never crowded."

"I'd love to," Kath said without hesitation. "Of course, I would."

"You know, I can't seem to get you off my mind," James Gordon, said after a moment, turning his eyes away. "I mean, it's not a bad thing. After my wife died, I shut a door in my heart. I shut it hard and locked it. But I woke up one morning and I found it hanging open a crack. It was almost like a dream and I wondered how that had happened. And when I pushed it open further, I saw you standing there."

"You don't think I'm going mad," do you," James Gordon said, after a moment of awkward silence.

"Oh no," Kath said, glancing across at him and reaching out to take his hand. "I know all about that door. Mine has opened too. And you're sitting here right next to me."

The next evening when James Gordon picked her up to go to the restaurant, however, the two of them acted as though there had not been that moment of open doors on the park bench the day before. In fact, Kath was afraid that the silence between them on the drive there might indicate that James was a bit sorry for what he had expressed the day before.

But she needn't have worried. Later at the restaurant after they had eaten and were drinking strong black tea from delicate china cups, Kath looked around her from where they were sitting in an intimate booth in the corner, at the bright Chinese silk gown that was hanging on the far wall. It was displayed between colorful framed photographs of China and Japan, of Mt. Fuji, and twin pagodas on a hill with cherry blossoms. James Gordon was staring too.

"Do you travel, Kath," he finally asked looking directly into her eyes. "I traveled all over the world when I was in the navy. I find I have a hankering to do a little of it again."

"I haven't traveled for years," Kath told him. "I went on a pilgrimage to England and Scotland a long time ago, and visited the homes of some of the English writers and Poets. Lately I've been bogged down a bit just traveling through life."

"I understand Kath," he said, and then was silent for an awkward moment before turning to her and going on. "I know it's been difficult, but if you let me, I'd like to come along with you. I don't know where the journey will take us, maybe nowhere. Maybe someday we could go on a real journey to somewhere far off like the places in those photographs. But for now, I'd like to travel along with you right here, one day at a time. What do you say?

Kath couldn't say anything at all. She just stared at him and didn't care if he saw the tears that were forming at the corners of her eyes.

Later that night after having a difficult time going to sleep, Kath had a dream. It was vivid enough that she would remember it for years. She was in the park lost in a blizzard. She was searching for Fred. She had lost him somehow and she cried out, calling his name. Suddenly there was Marcus in front of her. He took her arm and told her he would see that she got home. Then Cassandra was at her feet and the snow had stopped. And suddenly there was James Gordon in front of her and the snow was gone, and it was spring. And then just as she was about to open the door to the house, Fred was standing in front of her, smiling. "I'm sorry Kath," he told her. "I have to go back, but I heard you cry out and I helped you in the only way I could, I brought these others to walk with you and help you along. And it's okay. Love lasts, but you must realize it changes as we go. Another face, another hand, another life. Be happy with this life you still have ahead of you. One day our paths will cross again, you'll see."

Kath was suddenly awake, but she had come back to herself at the proper time when every detail of the dream was remembered. And she understood the imagery completely. And yet she was sure in her heart of hearts that it was truly Fred who had come to her and let her know that he had heard her cry out the night of the blizzard and that he had indeed set wheels in motion to help her out of the darkness. And he had also heard her that day in the cemetery and wanted her to know he had.

The bright days of sunshine returned, almost as quickly as they had gone, and Kath found herself thinking of Geraldine Harvey. It had been two or three weeks now since she had visited her in the hospital. Kath was watering the geraniums on the patio when the woman's face came to her so suddenly it was a bit of a shock. So much had happened, so much had been going on that she had stored more away in the closets of her mind than she realized.

Was Geraldine Harvey home from the hospital; was she even still alive? Twinges of guilt rose in her and she made up her mind that she would attempt to visit the woman the next morning, despite the worry that what she might find could be unpleasant. What did one take when visiting a sick woman? She had taken roses the day she had gone to see her in the hospital. Perhaps it might be a good idea to stick to flowers, a small geranium perhaps, since she had been tending her own when Geraldine Harvey's face flashed into her mind.

That afternoon Kath drove out to the nursery and located a small pink geranium in a colorful clay pot. The next morning, she carried it up the street to Geraldine Harvey's house. It was a splendid morning but there was a touch of fall in the air. The temperature was cool and pleasant, and the scent of Anderson's creek reminded her of how the world used to smell, fragrant, nostalgic, as she walked up to the college to work on those not so long-ago days. She would have to go back there again, she realized, and before long, but right now she had to see to Geraldine Harvey.

She arrived at the house, climbed the stairs and

knocked on the door. There was no sound from inside and Kath was suddenly afraid no one was there. Had Mrs. Harvey already succumbed? She knocked again and suddenly the door was opened by a tall middle-aged woman with graying hair. She was dressed in slacks and a blouse and she smiled when Kath told her she had come to see Mrs. Harvey and wondered if she was able to receive guests.

"She's not feeling so well this morning," the woman told her. "I'm her day nurse. I'll ask her first. And your name is?"

"I'm Kathleen Longley, her neighbor from down the street," Kath said. "She'll remember me I'm sure."

The lady went into the back and returned almost at once. "Yes, she'll see you," she said. "She called you Mrs. Lonely. Her speech, you know..."

"Yes, I know," Kath said. "I've always been Mrs. Lonely to her."

There was an antiseptic smell to the house as Kath followed the nurse though the living room and the hall where she had found the lady on the floor. At a bedroom in the back she found Mrs. Harvey in a wide double bed propped up by pillows. She was wearing blue pajamas and looked even thinner and paler than she had when she saw her in the hospital. Her hair had been combed into place, but her face was taut as though she were in pain.

"Oh, Mrs. Lonely," Geraldine Harvey said, her voice a bit weak, "you said you'd come."

"I brought you a geranium," Kath said, holding out the plant. "I thought you might like it."

Mrs. Harvey tried to grasp the pot, but it was obviously too heavy, so Kath made a spot for it on the bedside stand beside her, then sat down on the chair next to the bed.

"Pink is my favorite color," Geraldine Harvey said, holding out her hand, taking Kath's into it. "Thanks for bringing it to me. My mother loved geraniums. That's her in the picture there," she said indicating with a shaking hand the picture next to her on the stand.

Kath glanced for a moment at the photograph of a stout lady in a house dress standing on a porch somewhere, a hard-serious look on her face. She seemed to be wiping her hands on an apron that she wore over the dress.

"She worked herself to death," Geraldine Harvey said. "All day long, from morning to night, she worked. I worked too, but I got away from the farm. I met my husband in the shoe factory here in town. We worked hard too, but I at least had a life. We were poor, of course, but we managed to get this house. I have to be happy with what the good lord has given me."

Geraldine Harvey's mind wandered as she talked about her life and Kath listened quietly, until after what seemed a long time, she began to nod off. "I think I'd better be going now," Kath said then, "You need to get some rest. I'll come back..."

"Please do, please do..."

"Is there anything I can bring you when I come again," Kath asked, standing up. "Anything at all, food, another plant?"

"I was thinking about peaches," Geraldine Harvey said, her voice fading. "We always had peaches on the farm at this time of year. My mother always made a peach cobbler. I'd love one of those..."

"I'll fix one and bring it to you," Kath said quickly,

without thinking. "It may not be as good as the ones you remember but I'll bring it anyway."

Geraldine Harvey's eyes closed then, and Kath slipped from the room. The nurse was sitting on the sofa as she went into the living room.

"How is she really doing," Kath whispered before leaving. "Does she have much time?"

The nurse shook her head. "No, it's just a matter of days. She's sedated and on serious pain medication. I'm surprised she even knew who you were. Hospice will be here later. Mrs. Gillian has been coming every day. If you want to see her alive again, I wouldn't wait too long. She has very few friends."

Kath walked home in silence. The day was suddenly muted, the sun seemed dimmed. Of course the sudden cloud of depression had fallen due to Geraldine Harvey's condition, but what had she gotten herself into? Somewhere in her bookshelf or her files there had to be a recipe for Peach Cobbler. Fred had often told her she was a good cook, and sometimes she fancied herself as such, but she had to be in the mood for it and it had often helped that he had been there to help with the clean-up and especially the enjoyment of whatever it was she was fixing. In this case she would be preparing something for someone who she had only recently come to know, a kind of enemy who had only recently become a friend. It would be difficult to find the real cook within her. but she would give it her best. Mrs. Harvey had asked for Peach Cobbler, a strange request, in a web of stranger days, but she would do her best at fulfilling the request.

That afternoon she found the recipe and then drove to the market and collected the ingredients she would need. By evening the house was full of the delicious aroma of the cooked fruit and the cake-like topping. There was a moment as she stood at the counter waiting for the oven to do its work, that she almost reached out to find the small glass of white wine that had always been there when she cooked with Fred nearby. And that is where it really had started, she realized, the taste for alcohol. It had been an enjoyable pastime in the sunny days of her life, until the rains came, and it reached out with its dark web and tried to consume her. Now she was grateful that she could prepare the cobbler without the help of that elusive friend. And she didn't stop with just one cobbler, she fixed three smaller ones. One she would wrap and take to Mrs. Harvey the next day, another she would keep for herself. Perhaps Marcus would drop by later and even Cassandra could have a small sample. The last one, she decided in a sudden flash, she would take up the hill and deliver to James Gordon!

But time got away from her. It was nearly dark when she was finished with the cleaning and clearing. She loved the fixing of food, loved the mystery of bringing a dish into being, the organizing, the searching. She loved the aroma and usually the taste of the dish itself. But what she hated was the clean-up, the lost spoon or dish. How in the world did it get there? So that after her fixing of the cobblers she stood back and surveyed a clean and clear kitchen. She came back to herself completely when she heard Cassandra whine at the door and she went over and after switching on the outside lights went out on the patio while the dog went out and roamed round the yard for a moment before going to the gate and staring out. Kath knew she was looking for Marcus.

Kath had purchased a padlock for the gate and the evening she had taken to locking it. During the day the lock was left hanging on the fence. As she stood there, she realized she had not locked it that evening as she had become engrossed with her baking. Now the fact that she was left in the dark nearly unprotected, sent her quickly over to the gate where she snapped the lock into place. Here by the fence she had a clearer view of the sky with its myriad sea of stars, and the moon rising above the horizon. The scent of the summer air that hung over the park and crept down over everything, dark and mysterious and quite heady, held her in its grip. Above her on the hill she could see the lights of James Gordon's house and wondered what he might be doing at this moment. He would call her before he went to bed. He had taken to doing this just to see that she was okay. He would show up in the morning wanting to walk and she could give him the cobbler then. The thought of going outside the safety of the fence and across the street and up the stairs in the dark left her feeling afraid.

She was about to turn and go back to the house when Cassandra at her feet began to whine and the low sounds in her throat suddenly became a bark. A dark figure emerged from the shadows, walking quickly up the slope to the gate. Kath could tell at once that it was Marcus. But after retrieving the key to the lock from the house and allowing the boy inside she detected at once that something was wrong. Marcus walked with a limp and she picked up the sound that he was breathing heavily. Before she had a chance to ask him what was wrong, he went out into the yard with the dog.

It was only a few moments later when he came into

the house that Kath saw the black eye and the bruises on his face and arms, causing her to cry out. "What happened to you Marcus? Are you alright?"

At first Marcus ignored her, going into the living room with Cassandra, but finally he returned to the kitchen where Kath was preparing coffee at the counter. He sank into a chair and lowered his eyes. Kath took the two mugs of coffee she had fixed to the table and sat down opposite him.

"Now do you want to tell me about it," she asked. "Who did this to you? Your father?"

Marcus shook his head, and breathed deeply.

"When did this happen, Marcus?"

"This afternoon," he answered, and the sound of his voice told her something was wrong. He could barely get the words out, and he coughed and held his chest as though it caused him pain to speak.

Kath went into action at once. She got up from the table, went into the living room and grabbed her purse. "Come on, Marcus," she told him. "I'm taking you to the emergency room!"

"I don't want to go," the boy protested. "I'm okay..."

"You are not okay," she said firmly. "And there is no use being stubborn." Despite the anxiety that she suddenly felt rising in her own mind and body she took Marcus's arm and he had no choice but to go with her to the car. Once they were inside and were headed toward the hospital, she asked him again.

"Now who did this to you?"

After a long moment of silence Marcus finally spoke. "It was those boys over in the woods."

"Why would they beat you like this?" Kath asked. "I'm going to call the police when we get back!"

"No, you can't do that," Marcus protested his voice nearly a scream. "They threatened to kill me. They'll do it too."

"Why would they want to kill you!"

Marcus didn't answer, and Kath didn't question him again, since it was obvious, he was in pain. They rode the rest of the way to the hospital in silence. Once there, and after a long wait, and a difficult series of questioning and paperwork they were finally in a cubicle where a doctor took charge. He was middle aged and graying and wore glasses that had the thickest lenses Kath had seen in a while. He did preliminary testing of Marcus's blood pressure and reflexes, all the while questioning what hurt and what didn't. When he asked how the injuries had happened Marcus gave the same story that he had been climbing a tree to rescue a cat and had fallen when one of the limbs had broken. Kath had not protested and only shook her head slightly at the ease in which Marcus had told such a blatant lie. Her only thought was in having him checked out to see how seriously he was injured.

"He has a badly bruised chest and a broken rib," the doctor told Kath after Marcus had been put through a series of x-rays and blood work. We'll give him some pain medication and try to keep him calm for the next few days, and definitely keep him from climbing any more trees!"

"I don't think the doctor believed your story," Kath told Marcus when they were back home a couple of hours later. It was nearly midnight by this time and they were finally sitting at the kitchen table. This time Marcus was sipping on a coke and Kath was having iced tea.

"You shouldn't have lied to them," Kath said. "I kept quiet since I only wanted to get you well. Now let's have the truth. What happened?"

"I went over into the woods…"

"But you said you weren't going to go over there again…"

"I know," Marcus said, moving the coke can in circles on the table in front of him. "But I had to go over there again. It's the nightmares I've been having. But they seem real. And it's always the same thing where I look out the window and see a light going between the fence and the railroad embankment and I go out and follow it into the woods! I get close enough to hear someone crying out, almost screaming, and then I realize its one of those boys and he has a girl taking her back to their camp. I think it's that tall one. I try to get close enough to see who it is, but I trip over something and fall on my face. Before I can get up, I hear the girl scream and then everything is quiet. I reach down and feel a chain. I've tripped over some sort of chain. And then I wake up."

"But still, you shouldn't have gone over there…"

"I know, but I had to find out if there really was a chain," Marcus said, coughing again, as though in pain. I went in the afternoon when I thought no one would be over there. Everything was quiet and still, and I was quiet myself. And I found the chain! It was real. It was like a chain for a dog someone must have kept there at one time. I was examining it when they came out of nowhere and grabbed me. Two of them, that big one and his friend. I always see them together. They dragged me back to the camp and beat me up and told me never to come there again. If I did, they'd kill me! I told them

I knew what they did, and they beat me some more."

"But what did you mean, Marcus." Kath asked, her body tense. "What did they do?"

"Why they killed that girl!" Marcus cried. "My nightmare. It was real. I must have followed them that night. I tripped, and I didn't actually see them do it. But they did do it! And something else, Mrs. Longley. Those boys stole your furniture. I saw it there! It's sitting right in front of their shack!"

CHAPTER 14

The shock of what Marcus had told her sent Kath into a fit of coughing. Her anxiety came back to her in a rush and she almost got up and ran to find one of her pills. But instead she sat there keeping her hands steady and her wits about her. Much as she had been rattled by the boy's story, she felt it best not to let him see how deeply disturbed she really was. So, she sat staring at his face, quite pale and white in the artificial light from the ceiling.

Was he telling the truth? She couldn't come right out and ask him, nor could she come to her own conclusion if it was truth or lies. He had told lies to her in the past. Especially the one where his mother was still living at home. There were other instances of things being stretched a bit, but she could understand most of that. Young people sometimes had to deal with over active imaginations. But murder. That was something else again. And perhaps it had been a nightmare after all. The whole story had seemed dream-like to her. But what about the chain he had supposedly tripped over? And her furniture. Was that the truth or also a figment of the boy's imagination?

"Oh Marcus, you've been through quite a shock," Kath finally said, getting up from the table. "Why not just try to relax as much as you can right now and get some rest. I know your father will come after me but I'm not letting you go home tonight. You can stay here. You can sleep upstairs in the guest room or right in on the sofa. I'll make a bed for you there. Casandra will like that. Okay?

Marcus didn't protest, and after Kath went in and arranged a sheet and blanket on the sofa, she took the boys arm and led him into the living room. Cassandra, who had been lying peacefully at his feet, followed happily. Kath had a feeling the dog would not be sleeping upstairs with her tonight.

What in the world should she do about the situation, Kath wondered when she was finally settled down in bed for the night? Call the police and make a fool out of herself and Marcus? Yes, the boys had beaten him and should be turned in. And what of her furniture? Perhaps she should make a trip into the woods herself and see if they were the guilty party who had stolen it from her front porch. But for the time being she would let it all settle in her mind and perhaps in a day or two she would finally have the answers she needed and would take some sort of action. But right now, she had to concern herself with her own physical concerns and emotions so that she didn't suddenly veer off her own personal path.

Sleep finally came though she had no idea how long she lay there wrestling with her thoughts. She awoke finally to a gray morning, and peering out the window she saw that it was raining. Her spirits sank a bit hoping they were not in for another long siege of rain. There would be no walk with James Gordon that morning and the thought disappointed her. But not longer after she was in the kitchen having her first cup of coffee, he called her on the phone, which cheered her up again.

"I want you to come up to the house for dinner to-night," he said. "I remember you and Fred came up once long ago when my wife was still alive. Would you like that?"

"Oh, very much," she said. "And by the way I made some peach cobblers yesterday. There's one for you and I'll bring it with me. So, don't fix a dessert."

It was after ten before she was ready to deliver the cobbler she had made for Geraldine Harvey. Marcus had stumbled into the kitchen earlier along with Cassandra and they had gone out into the rain for a brief period. Inside again, Marcus had ended up back on the sofa asleep with Cassandra at his feet.

Kath took her largest umbrella and slipped quietly from the house. She had planned on walking to Mrs. Harvey's house, but the rain was coming down harder than before, so she decided it would be best to drive the short distance. The world was etched in lines of rain and fog as she maneuvered the car from the garage to the street. There was a slight chill in the air and the wind was stirring all the trees bringing sudden sheets of rain to the windshield.

Kath was able to park the car on the opposite side of the street and make it to Mrs. Harvey's door without getting too wet. She had worn a light sweater which helped, and the umbrella had been a bit of a nuisance, but she was glad she had brought it.

Mrs. Harvey's nurse had an anxious look on her face when she opened the door to Kath's knock. "She's bad this morning," she said. "I've called hospice and she'll be here soon. You can go in but I'm not sure she'll wake up. She's heavily sedated."

Kath gave the cobbler to the nurse and went quietly into the bedroom at the back. A small lamp was burning on the opposite side of the bed, and Mrs. Harvey lay quite still, a blanket pulled up to her throat. There was a peaceful look to her face, though her coloring appeared grayish. Kath had to look closely to see that she was even breathing. But she sat there for what seemed a long time, surveying the room. Her eyes took in the sparse furniture, the pink curtains at the windows and the scenes of cows and horses on the prints on the wall. Geraldine Harvey had lived frugally, it was obvious, but there were touches of home, the life she had lived on the farm.

Kath was sitting there quietly, trying to achieve a meditative state, when Mrs. Harvey's voice sounded suddenly causing her to sit up with a start.

"Is someone here?" the voice was weak but audible. The eyes flickered and then opened widely, appearing in the weak light as two very dark splotches on the pale skin.

"It's Mrs. Longley, from down the street," Kath told her. "I fixed you a peach cobbler. I wanted to bring it while it was still fresh."

"Bless you," Mrs. Harvey said, drawing out the words. "Can you bring me a little? I'd like to taste it again..."

Kath got up at once and went to find the nurse in the kitchen. Hearing of the woman's request, she carefully spooned some of the cobbler into a small dish and heated it briefly in a microwave. Once prepared, she handed the dish and a spoon to Kath.

"Back in the room Kath pulled the chair she had been sitting in close to the bed and touched Mrs.

Harvey's arm. "I have the cobbler here, Mrs. Harvey," she said. "Can I feed you a bite?"

"Yes, oh yes," Geraldine Harvey said, opening her mouth slightly with some effort. Kath dipped the spoon into some of the warm peach mixture and carefully lifted it to the ladies opened lips. She took it into her mouth with a pleased sound, and then opened her mouth again.

"It's so good," she said. "As good as my mother's and mine..."

Kath attempted to spoon another small bit into the lady's mouth, but Geraldine Harvey had slipped into unconsciousness. The nurse had been standing by the bed and took a damp cloth she carried and wiped her half-opened lips.

"I think she'll slip away soon, Mrs. Longley," she said. "All the signs are there."

Kath was silent. She realized she should just go away and let the old lady die in peace. After all they had been enemies of a sort for a long time. She had given the old lady something to focus her frustration, her anger on, and now close to the end they had come together in peace. But it had not been her doing, Kath realized. She had not attempted in any way to keep the feud going. And now at the end she didn't have the heart to walk away. The sadness of the situation lay in the fact that Mrs. Harvey had no one there with her to see her through the mysterious door that lay between life and death. But closing her own eyes for a moment of reflection, Kath imagined someone from the other side waiting on the other side of the door. Perhaps Mrs. Harvey's husband, or her parents. She had surely been loved. For on the other side of the hard wall the woman had built around herself, Kath detected hints of love and kindness.

A sound from the bed brought Kath back to herself. Looking down she saw that Mrs. Harvey's eyes had opened and she was looking up at someone, though it was not at her, she realized. She was looking directly above her at an invisible presence only she could see. And then words seemed to be forming in her throat, and she spoke. Though very faint, Kath heard everything she said.

"Old Mrs. Lonely knows... how to be kind."

And then after a moment, in which she seemed to have difficulty in clearing her throat, she spoke again, though even more faint, "Old Mrs. Lonely knows how to forgive." And with that her head seemed to drop and she was quite still. There were no more sounds from her chest and only complete silence from the bed.

Kath was weeping silently by this time. She wiped the tears from her eyes with her hand until the nurse who had been standing on the opposite side of the bed witnessing the scene handed her a tissue. Kath took it, slightly amazed that the nurse who had probably stood silently by while many others had exited their human lives, still seemed to have understanding and compassion. The woman was nearly in tears herself, Kath noticed, and she came around to where Kath was sitting, and lay her hand on her shoulder. "She's gone, dear," the woman whispered. "It was good that you were here. You can have peace knowing you did all you could."

Kath thanked the nurse and lay her hand on Mrs. Harveys silent ones before leaving the room. Later as she got in the car and drove back toward home, she did feel a kind of peacefulness drift over her. It wasn't that she had done much. She hadn't done anything at all, really. Perhaps she had just tried to do the right thing. Often in life it seemed that doing what you thought was right often turned out to be wrong. Two different people, two different views of a situation. And as far as Mrs. Harvey was concerned, it gave Kath a sense of peace knowing that even in the face of death she had done what was right after all.

The rain had slacked a bit by the time she arrived home. Hurrying inside Cassandra greeted her at once with a loud bark and a welcoming tongue. Marcus was gone. The sofa was empty, and the blanket and sheet had been neatly folded. Kath's spirits sank a bit knowing he had left before she got back. Of course, she had not told the boy she was going out, but now she would worry if he was going to be all right. The vial of pain pills the doctor had given him were still on the kitchen counter, and she had no idea when he would return. What reaction would his father have when he saw the black eye and the bruises? And what would he say and do when he realized Marcus had spent the night at her house?

There was too much to be thought of and worried over, Kath realized. She was suddenly quite tired and with a cup of coffee at hand she went into the living room and sank into her chair. She drank half the coffee, then sat it aside and wrapped herself in her afghan. Cocooned herself, really. It was one of those moments that she often had where she just wanted to be left alone, where she didn't want to do anything at all but just hide.

Kath fell asleep and it was afternoon when she woke up. The house was silent, and she lay there for several moments surveying her physical and mental selves. Marcus had obviously not returned, and Cassandra was asleep in her cage. Kath was a bit surprised that she felt as much in control of herself as she did. After the morning in which she had experienced Mrs. Harvey's death she would have thought her anxiety might return and cause her panic and discomfort. But somehow, she was healing from her sensitized state and no longer had that fear of slipping back into it again. She had taken the doctors advice and had adjusted the dosage of her medication just as he suggested, but she hadn't noticed any ill effects. She would never turn to the alcohol again. Even in another dark place, she would find another hand to hold as she made her way through the maze.

Cassandra finally stirred and came out of her cage and whined at her feet. Reluctantly, Kath emerged from the safety of her chair and afghan and went out with the dog to the yard. The rain had stopped by this time, but the sky was still a swirling mass of clouds. She longed for a clear summer night where she could stand in the dark and look up at the stars. Much as she liked the sound and look of the rain on the world, she had had her fill of rain. And there was a touch of Autumn on the world now. September would soon arrive, heralding a long stretch of road moving toward winter.

Precisely at six o'clock Kath took the cobbler and headed across the street and up the stairs and path toward James Gordon's house. She had dressed in a light blue dress and after fussing with her hair and nails, and adding a bit of makeup to her face decided she was presentable. Her thoughts had been on him during the long day, but she had kept them comfortably to one side. Now, climbing the stairs, he was all over her in a rush, and she felt a deep flush move across her cheeks. Twilight was falling by this time so perhaps he wouldn't notice she was blushing like a school girl.

James Gordon met her at the door and stood for a long moment staring at her. He was dressed comfortably in slacks and a green shirt, and even in the gathering dusk his blue eyes twinkled, and she had a sudden desire for him to kiss or at least hug her. But he simply held out his hand and took hers and led her into a wide hallway. He took the pan of cobbler from her and carried it off to the kitchen. The house was much larger than it appeared from the street, and from her memory of it, Kath noticed while she waited for him to come back. She and Fred had been invited a couple of times while Mrs. Gordon was still alive. A wide staircase led to an upper floor, and several closed doors led off to other sections of the house. The living room into which he led her when he returned was warm and comfortable. There was a nautical theme, large paintings of sailing ships adorned the walls, and several model ships were lined up on a large bookcase at one side of the room. A large window looked out on Bridgetown where lights were beginning to twinkle on. Kath could see her own house below, and had a vague thought that she wished she was safely back there where the magnetism of this man would not bother her quite as much. As she stood for a moment surveying the room, she wondered why James Gordon was still living there, it was obviously too much space for him.

As though sensing her thoughts, James Gordon came to stand next to her at the window. "This house is obviously too much for a single man like me," he said,

"I thought about selling the place after my wife died. But there wasn't anywhere else I wanted to be, so I just settled in and learned to live alone. So, I guess I'll just keep living as I am. And now I have..."

He stopped in mid-sentence and Kath was almost sure he was going to say "you," but instead he took her hand and led her back into the hall and out to the back patio. The wide expanse, comfortably furnished in white wicker furniture and large green ferns, looked out over the park. A table was lit by candles and sat near the back railing. It contained some colorful china plates and crystal glasses. James Gordon pulled out a chair for her, made her comfortable by offering her some iced tea which he poured from a pitcher.

Then he left her for a few moments while she sat and sipped at the tea. The darkness had fallen by this time and the scents of the evening, deep and earthy, rolled down from the park in the distance. A sudden wave of fear washed over her quite unexpectedly then. Was it the mystery of the deep summer night, with its myriad sounds, dogs barking and faint voices from far off? Or the deep woods beyond the park and the secrets they held? She was still trying to figure it out when James returned with the food.

"I hope you don't mind we're having spaghetti," he said. "I'm afraid my food repertory is rather lacking, and I always seem to stick to what is familiar."

Kath assured him she liked spaghetti very much, and in fact once she had tasted it declared it to be quite delicious. There was also a salad and warm French bread, and at the end James served the cobbler she had brought. He warmed it before bringing it to the table, and after taking a bite of it, said she could really cook!

It was a pleasant meal and James Gordon kept the conversation going. Once they were finished eating, they sat for a long time in silence. But it was not an uncomfortable quiet. It reminded her of long evenings spent with Fred in which there had been no words spoken at all. There had only been a feeling of comfort and satisfaction in the realization that you were living a shared life and there was nowhere else you wanted to be, or anyone else you wanted to be with.

Later as she was ready to leave James Gordon did give her a warm hug. "I'm so glad you came," he told her, and all Kath could think was that she wished he had held her a bit longer. His body had been so warm in her arms and old feelings had been awakened and tears had almost slipped from her eyes.

"We'll have more evenings like this one," he said, "I've enjoyed having you here more than you know. Now I'll walk you home."

They were about to go out the door when he stopped, turned to her and touched his forehead with his fingers. "Oh, I knew there was something I forgot to tell you. That girl. You know the one who was missing? Well she's back. I found out today. She was living in a cabin up in the mountains. She had a boyfriend and was pregnant..."

CHAPTER 15

Kath was so shocked she could hardly speak. Going down the stairs toward the street she was glad that James Gordon was holding onto her arm and that the darkness helped to hide the stunned look she must have had on her face.

There was an awkward goodbye at the gate and once inside the house where Cassandra danced at her feet, the full reality of what James had told her washed over her. The girl was back. She was safe. She had not been kidnapped or murdered. The boys in the woods were not guilty. "Oh Marcus," she whispered aloud, "How could you make up such a story? How can I ever trust you again?

Cassandra finally made her way to the door and Kath let her outside and stood at the edge of the patio in the dark while the dog wandered about the yard for a few moments. The only light came from the window and the open doorway and for once the darkness seemed to protect and cocoon her from the life that lay too close to her now. She supposed it should be one of those times where if she were going to turn to alcohol again to smooth the edges of the anxiety that was gathering around her like an army about to attack, this would be it. After all, in this one day she had stood by while a woman had died, had dinner with a man who she was growing a bit fonder of each day, and been deceived and lied to by a young man who she cared about and had attempted to help. Yes, it would be so easy to go down and retrieve one of the few bottles of wine from the cellar. But after several moments of breathing deeply of the cool night air, trying to detect and analyze the myriad layers of scent, she realized that it would be futile to take that road again. Too many pitfalls had lay along it and her rescue had come from her own cries in the dark. Perhaps the next time she would not be so lucky.

She had had many sleepless nights in her life, but the night that followed was a bit different in its depth and intensity. Thankfully, Cassandra had gone into her cage and curled up in the corner, so that when she did finally go upstairs, she went alone. And even with her jumbled thoughts, she was rescued by periods of sleep, each one haunted by dreams of trying to answer a question or solve a mystery. By morning, however, after waking up time and time again, she was washed up on a shore of wakefulness and finally decided to crawl from the covers and make her way downstairs.

What was she to do about Marcus? After her night of dreams and private detection, she realized this was a question that needed to be answered. But one thing she was sure of, she would have to draw a line in the sand with the boy. She could not go on trying to fix someone else when there was so much fixing that still needed to be done within herself.

Kath finally made her way into the kitchen and fixed some coffee, let Cassandra outside, and then stood at the door and watched as the sun came up over the park, a lovely sight after all the rain and mists of the past days. The sky was a brilliant blue and seemed to herald a better period, at least with the weather. But in her own mind she was not so sure. The atmosphere there was still cloud covered and unsure of itself.

She was standing there staring out when Cassandra began barking, and looking off to her left, Kath saw Marcus open the gate and slip into the yard. There had been so much on her mind the night before that she had forgotten to lock the gate. But somehow it wouldn't have mattered if a dark entity had entered and carried her off to a different world. Perhaps it might have been a peaceful place inhabited by people who had far fewer problems.

Marcus finally brought Cassandra into the house. He must have noticed right away that something was not quite right with Kath. By this time, she was sitting at the table clutching her coffee mug in her hands, and she didn't readily greet him with her usual cheery Good Morning. He stared at her and slipped into the opposite chair, the bruises on his arms and black eye seemed even more evident in the morning sun.

"Is something wrong, Mrs. Longley?" he asked. "You don't seem yourself this morning."

Kath was speechless for a moment. She had asked Marcus on several occasions to simply call her Kath, but the boy had never done so. There had always seemed that refusal to cross a line with her. Was it a fear of getting too close or simply a fear of her seeing the truth when he wanted to live in a world of imagination and lies? This morning his behavior angered her.

"We've got to talk, Marcus," Kath said finally, her voice sounding harsh. She cleared her throat.

"Do you remember I asked you once never to lie to me again?"

"Yes, I remember," Marcus answered, his face suddenly appeared fearful and taut.

"Then why did you lie to me about that girl being murdered?"

"What do you mean?" There was a shocked look on his face.

"Well, she came back. She's not dead, the boys didn't kill her."

"I don't understand? I saw..."

"Mr. Gordon just told me last night." Kath said, a bit angrily. "She was alive, living up on the mountain with a boyfriend. She was pregnant."

Marcus lowered his eyes in confusion. He rubbed his hands together nervously and then picked at one of his bruises.

But I know what I saw!" he said shaking his head.

"The girl is not dead, Marcus." Kath said. "If you accused them, that's probably why they beat you up."

"Well then they must have killed someone else," Marcus said, suddenly standing up, appearing confused and angry. "I saw what I saw. I'm sorry you don't believe me!" He went to the door then and just before opening it turned and looked at her hard. "You won't have to worry that I might lie to you again. I won't bother you anymore."

He left then, leaving Kath feeling weak and in tears. Cassandra rubbed hard against her legs and lay down at her feet, obviously realizing something was wrong. Had she been a bit too harsh with the boy, Kath wondered. And once again that old feeling seemed to haunt her, the feeling that everything in the world that went wrong was her fault. But perhaps she was simply trying to deal with her own anger. Was it wrong that she should be angry at Marcus who she simply had tried to help? But there was sadness too, no doubt due the fact that he had helped her, with all his flaws and blemishes, he had helped her come alive again. It was going to be a hard thing for her to accept that he seemed to be gone from her life.

And they were difficult days. Kath tried to keep busy. She secretly hoped that Marcus would suddenly show up again. Cassandra too, seemed to wait for him to appear, and seemed to be sadder as time passed that the boy didn't return. She took to spending more time in her cage and Kath became a bit worried.

One morning, while sitting on her front porch watching the increased traffic coming and going on the service road to the college, she decided that the perhaps the time had come for her to make her trip up there once again. It was September now and she had been spending more time on the front porch lately since it seemed easier to face life now if she stared in a new direction. She had taken to bowing out from the morning walks with James Gordon, since walking in the park seemed to remind her too much of Marcus. If the classes had not started yet, they would be starting soon. She was beginning to see students in pairs or alone walking along the streets of town.

Of course, when she thought about the inevitable visit up to her old classroom, the anxiety always seemed to increase. Mr. Sterner's face would rise before her and she would step back saying nothing. But as she had gotten into better control of herself, she imagined standing firmly before him and letting him know what she really felt, letting the anger rise in her so that it could eventually slide off her back and drift away. In the past weeks she had faced and dealt with so many issues, her addiction and anxiety, a terrible neighbor, a feud with a woman she hardly knew, and a final acceptance of her husband's death. Dealing with her nemesis up at the college seemed to be the next issue to be dealt with on her mental list. As in the other issues she had dealt with in order to get a better footing in her journey of life, the result might not turn out as she imagined, but facing and accepting seemed to be the key to dealing with old obstacles.

On a blazing September morning, a couple of days later, Kath left the house and crossed the street. She had dressed neatly in a comfortable dress and sweater, as the temperature was a bit cool. She stopped momentarily while crossing the bridge and looked down at the stream. It was still as clean and clear as she remembered, and its song as it moved over the moss and rocks below was familiar. But somehow, she did not recall it moving at this speed. It seemed to her that, like life, it moved faster and faster as time passed.

Kath moved on then, turning her attention to familiar vistas as she walked. Fanning out before her were the dorms and social halls. In the center, to which all streets came together, were the chapel and the administration buildings. Off to one side and closest to town were the buildings that housed the departments of learning and the classrooms. This morning there were students everywhere, moving in familiar patterns. She could hear bits of conversation and laughter. But no one seemed to notice too much that Kath was there. She was no doubt seen as just another professor showing up for work. As she neared Big Oak Hall where she had taught for many years, she suddenly realized that classes might be in session already and that her chance of confronting Robert Sterner might not be possible.

But there seemed to be almost total silence as she went into the building. Going along the hallway she was shocked that the only sounds coming from the place was a kind of distant hum. Did it come from the walls, or the machinery that caused air to flow, or from the building itself, whispering of all the lost years or the students who had passed in and out? Or perhaps it spoke to her though she wasn't sure what it was saying. Who are you? What are you doing back here? She hoped it was saying, Welcome back, I missed you.

Suddenly she was standing at the door to her old classroom, and taking a deep breath she reached down and turned the knob. There was a familiar squeak as the door opened, and Kath stood for a moment looking in. The room looked exactly as she remembered. The same white walls, the same dusty looking tables and desks. Her own desk seemed to sit in a pool of light though she was not sure where the light might be coming from as there were only a couple of small windows at the back leading to the outside. The only things that were missing, where the prints and objects she had used to brighten the place up a bit. The bookshelves to one side were nearly empty, as most of the books that had inhabited them had been hers. They were stored now along with the other things in her basement. Now she realized it may have been selfish of her to have taken it all with her when she left, but leaving it behind for Professor Sterner had seemed out of the question at the time.

Kath was standing there looking about the room when she heard footsteps in the hallway. They stopped suddenly, and when the door opened, a strange woman entered. She moved a few steps into the room but stopped, a bit startled when she saw Kath standing there. She appeared to be a few years younger than Kath and was smartly dressed in a longish green dress and a matching sweater. Her dark hair was long and appeared slightly damp. She was carrying a fat briefcase.

"Is there something I can do for you," the woman asked, after a moment of awkward silence. "I'm Julia Benton. I'm an English professor. I teach in this room."

"I'm sorry I've startled you," Kath finally said, moving closer and extending her hand. "I'm Kathleen Longley, this used to be my classroom. I came back..."

"Mrs. Longley!" Oh yes, you're the lady who left the letter!"

"The letter?"

"Yes, in the bottom drawer of the desk. I opened and read it!"

The woman turned quickly and walked to the desk at the front of the room where she lay down her briefcase. Rummaging in the bottom drawer of the desk, she retrieved an envelope and brought it back to where Kath was standing, and held it out to her.

Kath took it, her hand shaking a bit, and quickly read the inscription on the front. It was easy to recognize her own handwriting. And then it all came back to her in a rush. It was her last day as a teacher. All her things had been removed and she was making a last inspection of the place to be sure she had gotten everything. She was very hurt and angry at that moment and suddenly decided she wanted to say something, to let Robert Sterner know in a subtle way just what he had done to her and how she felt. So, she took out an envelope and blank piece of paper from one of the drawers and wrote down some thoughts that suddenly came to her mind.

Kath lifted the flap of the envelope and took out the folded sheet inside. "To anyone who may teach in this room," it said. "May you know the same challenges, the same fears and heartaches, the same competition I have had here. May you experience the same critical eye, the same demanding supervision. This may move and shake you, but, in the end, it will make you a stronger and better person and lead you toward the joys and happiness of a full and miraculous life."

Kath shook her head and returned the letter to the envelope. "Oh, I am so sorry you had to read that," she said. "It was really meant for Mr. Sterner. At the time I thought he would be the one to teach here. The one to find the letter and read it. I was sure he was going to exchange rooms. This one was the largest you see, and it has the private office behind the desk..."

"Oh, don't be sorry," Miss Benton said. "The letter inspired me. It helped get me through those first difficult months. I understand completely. He was a tyrant!"

"Was a tyrant?"

"Yes, haven't you heard? He's not here anymore. He left before the term ended in the spring."

Kath shook her head and felt as though she needed a place to sit down. Miss Benton took her arm and led her to an empty chair next to the desk. When they were both seated, Kath was finally able to speak again.

"What happened? I thought he would die here," she said.

"Well, apparently he must have thought so to," Miss

Benton said, rubbing her hands together and lowering her voice. "It was all hush hush. There must have been complaints from some of the other faculty and from the students. Touching, you see, unwanted advances. It must have all added up."

"Oh, that's hard to believe," Kath said. "He never showed me any of that. He was always breathing down my neck, but it was always something quite unnecessary and picky. Looking back, it seems like there was a deep insecurity there."

"That's exactly what it was. At first, I didn't think I wanted to stay here, but your letter helped me more than you know. Mrs. Thompson was made the department head after he was gone. Do you remember her? She's a bit wacky at times but so easy going and likeable."

"Yes," Kath said. "I liked her too. She was happiest going through stacks of books and reciting Chaucer."

"There was just some leftover anger in me," Kath said, staring at the desk where she had spent so many hours of work. "I wanted to lay it at his feet, to let him know how much his behavior had hurt me. That's why I came up here this morning."

"I'm sorry you didn't have that chance. Perhaps you can be glad with me that he's gone."

"Oh, I am so glad for your sake," Kath said, laying her hand on the desk. "And I'm happy I left when I did. I was able to spend a few happy months with my husband before he died. And we were very happy..."

Behind them a door opened just then and looking back Kath saw a young girl enter and sit down at one of the desks.

"My first class will be starting in a few moments,"

Miss Benton said. "Perhaps you can come up again some day soon. We can have lunch."

"I'd like that very much," Kath told her, standing up.

"And as for the letter, it will go right here in the bottom of the desk where you placed it. When I'm overwhelmed or discouraged, I'll take it out and read it again."

Kath thanked her, shook her hand and left the room quickly. Making her way through the throngs of students who had gathered on the campus, she made her way back toward her bridge and familiar street. As she walked, she thought it quite ironic that life had such a way of surprising us when we least expected it, how one street led to another, one avenue became wider, or narrowed a bit. So many people in recent times spoke of karma and how it was all knowing, that it would always take care of things, that the universe, the great God of wisdom, would work things out in its way. Nearing home, just as she was about to cross the bridge and the pure cold water that ran beneath it, she seemed to believe more than ever that the whole thing was true. Life would turn out as it would. It was most important, she realized, that we just did the best that we could, every moment, every day of our lives.

CHAPTER 16

The September days that followed were complete perfection as far as the weather was concerned. The sun shone from a flawless sky and there were few clouds. The summer heat was gone and had been replaced by a comfortable coolness in which Kath felt cocooned in a physical feeling of bliss. She spent many mornings on the patio trying to allow that perfect sense of peace into her brain and soul. But her mental weather was quite stormy. No matter where she might be, and she tried getting out as much as she could, she would imagine the sound of waves crashing against the shore of her world, threatening to wash away all the progress she had made against the onslaught of fear and anxiety that had threatened to send her into the deep.

And of course, there was a distinct feeling of loss and of failure. She missed having Marcus around and every morning and evening while she sat on the patio, she kept her eye on the gate hoping he would appear. What could she have done differently? She should have tried to comfort him that last night, told him she understood, that no matter where his story had come from, she would help him sort it out. Instead she had sat silently when he ran off in confusion and anger. And she hadn't expected that. So, she needed to understand that there are some things that can turn out badly despite all our efforts and desires for better outcomes.

James Gordon was a big help. She had taken to walking again. Sometimes they walked in the park and at others he drove them to a nearby lake where they walked on a path that encircled it. Cassandra went along and always enjoyed the wildlife, the ducks and geese that inhabited the water in profusion. But Cassandra had also gone into a depression of her own. She ate and drank as she always had, kept to her own routine. She loved the walks and her companionship with Kath, but it was obvious she missed Marcus. And why not? He had been her rescuer and her friend. She would lay on the patio staring at the gate. Inside the house she would listen to every sound and then stare at Kath as though asking where the boy was and why he wouldn't come to her.

One morning when she and James Gordon were sitting on their favorite bench at the top of the first hill, with Cassandra at their feet, he gave her a long hard look. "There's something bothering you, isn't there Kath? You haven't been yourself lately. It's Marcus, isn't it?" Kath had told him days earlier everything there was to tell about the Marcus situation.

She was silent for a moment staring down at the grass and macadam. "Yes, I'm very worried about him. I expected him to come back by now. I should have tried harder to understand. He's troubled and obviously needs some professional help. I'm willing to provide that."

"But he has a father Kath. You have to realize he's the one who has to help his own son."

"But he may be abusing the boy. I'm still not sure he isn't the one who beat him..."

"You know you could put an anonymous call into Children and Youth," James said, reaching out to take her hand. "They would come and take a look at the situation."

"Yes, I've thought about that. But his father would suspect I was the one who made the call and that could make things worse for Marcus and me."

James was quiet for a moment, gently massaging her hand in his. "You could go to him," he finally said. "Pick the right moment when the father's gone and then knock on the door. See if he answers."

That night, lying sleepless in bed, Kath went over in her mind what James had said. Should she do that? Could she? She was trying at all costs to avoid a confrontation with Bart Warner. She knew instinctively he could be violent. And yet she remembered on that last visit he had seemed afraid when she had stood up to him. Perhaps he was all threats and hot air after all. In the end she decided to think of doing what James Gordon had suggested. Perhaps she would work up the courage to attempt it.

The weather changed as the days stepped into October. It grew cold and the leaves began to morph, subtly at first and then more quickly as the days passed. The park became painted at the edges with rich colors of russet and gold. Across the street the maples were touched by splashes of yellow and orange. And then one morning, the sun was hidden behind dark rolling clouds and the wind whipped at the world. Kath realized, staring out the window just after letting Cassandra outside, that she would soon have to act. And that to-day would be as good a day as any to do so.

She dressed warmly in slacks and a jacket and then left the house making sure Cassandra was locked safely inside. She wanted to protect her in case there could be a possible meeting with Marcus's father. Who knew what the dog might do if caught in an unexpected situation.

Outside, the weather was a bit chilly but not as bad as it had appeared from the window. The wind was a nuisance but not violent. Kath left the gate and walked at a steady pace up the street toward Marcus's place. From the curve of the street near the entrance of the park she could stare further along toward the distant tunnel, at the edge of the railroad embankment where the mobile home was located. But she could not see any vehicles that might be parked there. It was only later when she had gotten a bit closer that she saw the tail end of the old green pickup truck sticking out from the bushes.

Kath's spirits fell. Perhaps things might not work out as she had wanted. She walked back to the park entrance and went inside. Just skirting the fence, she walked along it until she found a picnic table in a se-cluded spot from which she could just barely see the truck sticking out from the bushes. A look at her watch told her it was ten o'clock. Minutes passed and then nearly half an hour. She sat quite still but was filled with a sinking feeling. She was just about ready to go back toward home defeated, when staring down the street she heard a loud engine start up and saw the truck emerge from the bushes and back into the street and then move forward into the tunnel.

She was on her feet at once and headed back toward the park entrance and the street. A few minutes later she was standing looking at the mobile home, the first time she had looked at it closely. It appeared silent, cold and empty. She had a hard time imagining Marcus living inside. And what if he wasn't there? What if his father had really sent him away as he had often threatened? Kath moved into the yard and mounted the squeaky stairs. Her breath caught in her throat as she lifted her arm and knocked on the door, the sound on the faded metal loud and hollow.

There wasn't a sound from inside and she knocked again. Not wanting to walk away in defeat she knocked again a third time, this time even louder. Suddenly there was a metallic click from inside and the door opened. Marcus stood there and stared at her. His bruises and black eye were gone, and his eyes were wide with surprise.

"Mrs. Longley! What are you doing here?"

"Marcus, I've missed you and have been terribly worried about you. Are you alright?"

He was silent and lowered his eyes.

"Why haven't you come around? Cassandra is very sad and depressed. She's waiting for you to come back."

"You didn't believe me. You called me a liar again. I didn't think you wanted bothered anymore."

"Oh, Marcus I'm sorry. I was upset. But I want you to come back. We'll get you help..."

"I don't need help!" Marcus was suddenly angry. Kath saw it in his face, the way he clenched his jaw and closed his eyes. "I wasn't lying. Everything I told you that night was the truth!"

"Can I come in for a moment, Marcus?" Kath said

in a pleading voice. "I saw your father leave. Will he be back soon do you think?"

Surprisingly, Marcus moved aside, and Kath stepped in. "I don't know where he went," he said. "He may be gone for a few minutes or all day for all I know."

Kath was silent then as she looked about. The mobile home was small but neatly kept. She could see a small kitchen at the front of the place and she was standing in a living room with a sofa and an easy chair, a television and what looked like a stereo.

"Come with me," Marcus said then. I'll show you my room."

Kath nodded and followed the boy as he moved into a narrow hallway beyond the living area. She was quite surprised but relieved since the first reaction Marcus had shown when seeing her was hostility. The room Marcus led her to at the right side of the hallway was small but surprisingly well kept. There was a single bed and a desk in the corner which held a computer, a working one obviously, since the screen was lighted with a picture of a dog that looked very much like Cassandra. A bookcase sat nearby, filled with a large assortment of books and what looked like CD's or DVD's. On the wall were posters of animals, an elephant, a tiger and a smaller one of wolves.

"This is nice," Kath said, looking about. "Are you keeping up with your lessons?"

"For the most part," Marcus answered. "I've been reading, keeping to myself."

"Has your father been treating you okay?"

"Much better now that he knows I'm not coming to your house."

"But I want you to come back, Marcus. I care about

you and miss you. Why does he think its wrong for us to be friends?"

"He's afraid of something," Marcus said. "He's told me over and over that I'm not to confide in you, tell you my secrets. But I don't have any secrets. I don't know what he means. I don't pay any attention."

"But will you come back Marcus? "Kath said then, suddenly laying her hand on his shoulder. "For Cassandra's sake. For my sake?"

"I'll only come back if you let me take you into the woods and prove to you that I wasn't lying," Marcus said finally and firmly. "I wasn't lying about the chain or your furniture. Maybe it wasn't that particular girl who was murdered but someone was. I know what I saw."

"I'll go there with you Marcus," Kath said, her heart sinking even as she said it. Her anxiety and fear started to rise even as the words rose from her throat. The woods were dark and deep and obviously held a primal fear for her. "But when, when will we go."

"Right now." Marcus said, grabbing a jacket that was lying across a chair in the corner. "Before he comes back. Before you change your mind!"

Kath followed him out of the trailer. Outside the wind was still whipping at the trees and the leaves were falling, being swept across the street in sheets. The autumn scents were deep and pungent. Directly across from the trailer Kath could see where the chain link fence began, right at the edge of the railroad embankment. Marcus hurried across the street and squeezed into the opening. A narrow path led away into the underbrush. They were only a few yards along the fence when from behind them Kath heard Marcus's father's truck returning. It grew louder as it moved out of the tunnel and pulled into the driveway. Marcus stopped, and looked back, his face taut and pale.

"Do you think he can see us," Kath whispered, her voice almost indistinguishable above the wind and the rustling of the leaves.

"I don't think so," Marcus whispered. "But you go on and I'll go back and see what he's up to. Just go along this path and it will lead you to the camp. I'm sure there's no one there now."

"Are you sure, Marcus. I'm scared."

"It will be alright, Mrs. Longley. I'll come back shortly and find you. I promise."

Marcus moved away from her quickly and disappeared. Kath stood looking ahead of her at the faint trail that led through the dense thicket. The Autumn coloring normally would have filled her with a sense of awe, the beauty of the changing season almost too much to bear. Now there was only mystery and sadness, the terrible realization of something she had to face.

Kath moved along the trail, finding it hard going with the vines and briars that reached out to snag her clothes and scratch at her hands. Fallen trees and outcroppings of rock occasionally barred her way, but with care she made her way around them and moved further into the dense woods. Above her the tree limbs seemed to reach for her and threaten her sanity. Even the bright colors of Autumn failed to lighten the dark tunnel she struggled through. It seemed hard to breathe and she could hear her own heartbeat at times, when the wind slowed a bit and the leaves settled momentarily.

Stopping for a moment at one point to catch her

breath, she wished Marcus was still with her. He had been like a guide to her, not only today, but ever since the day he had first come to help her through the wilderness of snow and ice and anxiety. And he had helped her, more than she had ever realized before.

"What have I gotten myself into," she wondered. It suddenly felt to her as if she was caught in a web from which she would never escape, and out there somewhere was a monster waiting to devour her soul. She felt helpless for a moment and then suddenly the woods opened, and she stood in a kind of clearing. Looking down, she saw at her feet a rusty looking chain attached to a tree. It was obviously the one Marcus had tripped over!

Looking off to her left she saw through the undergrowth what appeared to be a dark mass, a building of some sort. Was it the camp the boys had built? Taking a deep breath, she made her way toward it. Here the path became clearer and in only a few moments she was standing right next to the ramshackle place. It was located right against the dark line of the railroad embankment, and sitting there in plain sight was her furniture! She recognized it at once, the sofa and misshapen chair and the small table that leaned to one side that had sat on her front porch for as many summers as she could remember. The boys had stolen it after all. Her neighbor was not the thief and Marcus had not lied!

Now what was she to do about it? Anger rose in her and she knew when she got back home, if she made it back, despite Marcus's protests, she would call the police and have them sort the whole thing out. But right now, where was Marcus? He had promised to return, and she had seen all she needed to see in this cursed place. Should she go back the way she had come or try to find the trail and the fence again and move to the end of the fence at the other end of the park? She suddenly decided that the latter might be the best course and she moved quickly toward the clearing where she had found the chain.

Beyond that she found the path again. It was very faint, but it was easier to follow now since she could make out the fence at times off to her right. She had gone a short distance, carefully moving through a deeper thicket of vines and briers when a flash of color drew her eyes to the left. It appeared to be a bed of flowers, with colors of red and yellow, very much out of place against the darker background. She stopped for a moment and stared at it, then moved closer, and pushing aside branches and bushes she saw that what she had noticed was actually a large display of plastic flowers, the kind of thing you saw in a cemetery that was used to decorate the graves...

Kath moved closer and saw that the unnatural bouquet sat at the end of a cleared area that looked very much like a final resting place. Had someone buried a pet here at one time perhaps? Is that what the chain had been about? But no, the plot was sunken and grave-like, far longer than it was wide. And with her heart beating wildly, Kath realized this was surely the grave of what had once been a human being!

She stood there for a long moment, wanting to hurry away from the place, but above and all around her the wind rose to a roar and seemed to hold her to the spot. Finally, it died for a moment and she was able to move away from the grave, even though her arms and

legs seemed paralyzed and she was driven by an invisible force outside herself.

"Where do you think you're going?"

The voice seemed to come from nowhere and sounded quite loud against the staccato of the rustling leaves
and the wind. Kath had been so engrossed at staring at
the flowers and what was obviously a grave, that she
had not heard anyone approach. She turned suddenly,
quite startled, and saw Marcus's father standing a short
distance off to her left. He was breathing so deeply she
could see his chest moving and his face held a look of
pure hate. He carried a long black object in his hand.
Was it metal? It reminded her of a tire iron.

"You had to nose around until you found her, didn't
you?" He said. "I knew you would. He told you, didn't
he?"

"I don't know what you're talking about!" Kath
managed to get the words out.

"Oh, you know alright!" Bart Warner said, his voice
nearly a scream. "You know that's my wife's grave and
that I killed her."

"Why I know no such thing," Kath said, the realization of what he was saying caused her to suddenly
feel as though she would faint. But she breathed deeply
and tried to get control of herself, thinking of what she
should do next. Should she run, certainly not the best
idea since she wouldn't get far in this underbrush.

"Yes, it's her grave," He went on. "And I'll put you
right next to her. There's enough space. You couldn't
leave well enough alone, could you?"

He moved toward her lifting the metal object in his
right hand. Terror paralyzed her, even caused her to
close her eyes. Her mind was blank, certainly not what

one would expect when you were about to die. She was waiting for a final crush of her skull when another voice cried, "Leave her alone!"

It was Marcus! Kath opened her eyes and in a kind of scene from a television drama, saw Bart Warner turn toward his son who had obviously sneaked up behind him, and saw the baseball bat in Marcus's hand raise up and slam into the side of his father's head. Bart Warner let out a muffled scream and fell to the ground with a loud thud.

Kath was suddenly frozen to the spot. The realization of what she had witnessed made her feel for a moment that she would pass out.

"Come on Kath," Marcus had dropped the bat was suddenly standing next to her grabbing at her arm. "We've got to get out of here!"

Marcus had called her Kath! The shock of that along with the scene she had just witnessed unleashed her adrenaline and gave Kath her strength back. She followed Marcus quickly, moving onto the trail again, and back the way they had come.

"He saw me come out of the woods," Marcus told her, breathlessly as they moved along through the thicket. "In the house he smelled your perfume and guessed you were in the woods with me."

"Did you know he killed your mother," Kath asked.

"I guess I always knew it at the back of my mind, but I didn't want to accept it. When that girl went missing, I started to have the nightmares and the truth began to come out." He stopped for a moment, as they both needed to catch their breath. "I realize now I followed my parents into the woods that night. They'd been fighting. He hit her in the house and I heard him say he was going to kill her. I must have blanked out when I tripped over the chain and fell on the ground. When I woke up the next morning, he told me my mother had left us. The past few days it's all started to come back and make sense.

"Oh Marcus, I'm sorry." Kath said. "I should have realized... But I had so much going on in my own life..."

"You've been good to me. That's enough."

Marcus took her arm and moved on quickly. "We've got to get back to your house. I don't know if he's dead. But if he is, he deserves to be and I killed him!"

Kath was exhausted when they arrived back at the gate. It had been a hard flight out of the woods. She had looked back several times half expecting Marcus's Dad to be following, but there was no sign of him. Marcus had been strong, helping her over many of the rough spots, but back in her yard, he sank into one of the chairs, breathing hard. Kath opened the door and Cassandra rushed past her wailing and half landed in Marcus's lap.

Kath grabbed the phone at once and called the police. She was surprised that she so easily related the whole situation to the 911 operator. He assured her, after taking her address, that they would be there momentarily.

"They're coming right away, Marcus," she told him. He got up from the chair and came to her. He was suddenly crying, and she cradled him in her arms. Cassandra was nearly wrapped around their feet.

"Don't let them take me away," he said. "I want to stay here with you and Cassandra. I need you Kath."

"I will do everything I can to make sure that you stay right here with me." She told him. "It may be easy, and it may be hard, but we'll face whatever comes together." Kath was suddenly crying, and she did nothing to try to stop the tears that had suddenly washed across her face. "Because Marcus, I need you, much more than you know. You are like a son to me."

"And you're just like my mother, kind and good."

Suddenly from a distance a siren sounded, and Kath held Marcus even closer. As the sound grew louder Kath saw James Gordon come hurrying down his stairs on the other side of Park Street, obviously alerted by the sound of the siren. Seeing them there, he entered the yard and rushed over and surrounded them both in the protection of his arms, just as the police car pulled up along the fence.

"What happened, Kath," he asked, his voice loud against the sirens wail.

Kath tried but couldn't answer. Her throat was so dry she wondered if she could ever speak again, and the anxiety she was feeling seemed likely to squeeze the last breath out of her. Marcus was shaking his head and sobbing. Kath wrapped her arms around him as tightly as she could, hoping her remaining strength would save the both of them.

When he got no answer, James remained calm and watched as two uniformed policemen hurried through the gate and rushed toward them.

"It's going to be okay," he whispered then. "Everything will work out."

CHAPTER 17

Kath was to remember that day on the patio, vividly, a few weeks later when she once again stood holding both Marcus and James Gordon close to her. It was a cold and dark day in late November and they stood on the far edge of the hill at the Memorial Gardens. The sky was covered with swirling clouds and all the trees were free of their leaves, a few of them appeared to her to be bowed down and weeping. Both Kath and James were misty eyed, and Marcus was crying soundlessly, his face burrowed in Kath's warm jacket. His mother's remains had been collected from her crude grave in the woods and brought there for a proper burial. A local priest had come and prayed and read some verses from the Bible, and his deep voice sounded hollow in the cold afternoon light. It was a difficult moment for Kath because of Marcus, who was obviously very much affected by the brief ritual. She had never met Marcus's mother, but she felt great empathy for the woman. And there had been too much death and pain lately, and she had come quite close to death herself, but had survived thanks to Marcus's quick action.

Thankfully, Marcus's father had not died from the bat hitting his head and dropping him to the ground. He was still unconscious when the police went into the woods and found him lying very close to his wife's grave. He was taken to the hospital and was diagnosed with a severe head injury. A few days later when he had come awake and was conscious, he was charged with murder and taken to the local prison to await a trial.

That afternoon with the graveside service behind them, Kath sat at the kitchen table sipping some coffee, and once again picked up and went over the newspapers she had saved. The headlines were large and stark against the white newsprint. LOCAL MAN KILLS WIFE AND BURIES HER BODY IN THE WOODS. In another, JUVENILE FELLS FATHER WITH BASEBALL BAT PREVENTING ANOTHER MURDER. And in the same paper, but lower down on the front page, a smaller headline read LOCAL GANG OF TEENS ARRESTED FOR BEATING A JUVENILE, and later the story told of their petty thievery of, among other things, a local woman's lawn furniture. The oldest of the gang, the article read, would be going to a juvenile prison for that and other criminal acts he had been involved in over the past couple of years.

She was sitting there going over the whole affair in her mind when the kitchen door opened, and Marcus and James Gordon came in. Kath got up from her chair to help since they were both burdened by the boxes and bags they were carrying. James was balancing two rather large boxes and Marcus held a large bag in one hand and had a colorful looking flat box under his other arm. Kath took the box from him, a picture puzzle of the faces of a lioness and her cub, and the smaller of the two boxes from James.

How did you make out," Kath asked as she followed them into the hall? "Did you get everything?"

"Yes," James said. "This is the last of Marcus's

things. The rest went to the auction barn. The mobile home is empty now and the railroad is going to see to the removal since it's partly on their property."

Marcus was silent, obviously still sad from the earlier event at the Memorial Gardens. He had gone up the stairs first, followed by Cassandra, who had been asleep in the living room when they arrived, and was very excited since she hadn't seen Marcus since that morning. He opened the door opposite Kath's office at the top of the stairs and went inside. Kath and James followed. The room had once been the guest room, but Kath couldn't remember a single guest who had ever spent the night there. It was three times the size of the small room Marcus had lived in at home, but glancing about the place she saw that it was very similar in the way Marcus had arranged it. The bed was part of the room and bigger of course, but the desk, the computer, the table and the bookcase had been brought with the help of James and a friend from Marcus's old room the previous week. In the corner was a new addition, Cassandra's cage. But Kath doubted the dog would spend much time in it. The nature painting of a stream and a covered bridge was above the bed as it had always been, but Marcus's animal posters, filled the rest of the walls.

Kath and James sat down the boxes leaving it up to Marcus to unpack what they contained. Marcus himself had sat down on the edge of the bed, looking sad and detached. For a moment he seemed to be staring into space. Kath sat down beside him suddenly and placed her arm around his shoulder. She handed him the puzzle.

"Are you alright, Marcus?" She asked. When he

OLD MRS. LONELY KNOWS

didn't answer she remembered telling him that what
the future held might be hard or easy but that they
would get through it together. She realized the hard
part had been Marcus's adjusting to the reality of his
mother's death. The easy part had been in being grant-
ed temporary guardianship of him. Kath had hired a
local attorney, Maude Smith, a very efficient and kind
woman, who had gotten them through all the red tape
and into the judge's quarters where the decision was
quick and official. After a few months Mrs. Smith
would begin the process of adoption. Kath had insisted
that Marcus himself see Dr. Barker and her counselor,
Jennifer Winston.

"You'll be fine, Marcus," James said, sitting down
on the other side of him and patting his back. "Isn't this
a splendid room Kath has given you? You're even going
to have a new TV soon, I understand."

After a moment Marcus nodded his head and sat
looking down at the puzzle he held in his hand. "My
mother gave me this puzzle for Christmas one year
and I put it away in my closet. Now I'm going to put it
together."

"That's great," Kath said. "When it's done maybe we
can preserve and frame it and hang it above the bed. It
is a beautiful picture and worth saving."

Kath stood up then and James followed. Marcus
stood too, long enough to pick up Cassandra and place
her on the bed where they both lay down, Marcus closing his eyes and Cassandra snuggling close to him.

"You have a good rest now," Kath said as she was
about to leave the room. "I'll call you when dinner's
ready."

Marcus opened his eyes just as Kath put her hand

on the door handle. "Thank you, Kath, for everything," he said. "You know I'm going to go back to regular school next year. I want to study and work hard. I've decided when I'm through school I want to become a veterinarian like Dr. Riley. I know that would make my mother happy."

"I'll do everything I can to help you, Marcus," Kath said. "I know you can do it."

She left the room quietly, tears in her eyes. James followed but insisted he go down the stairs first in case she might lose her step. As she slowly followed him down, she thought of all the pieces of her own life that had been put into place in the last few months. The puzzle was not completed yet and perhaps it never would be, or beautiful enough to be framed and displayed. But looking below her to where James had reached the bottom and was staring up at her with a smile on his face, she realized the joy of life came from the slow process of putting each puzzle piece into place, one by one.

CPSIA information can be obtained
at www.ICGtesting.com
Printed in the USA
BVHW081907250920
589529BV00003B/11